TUSKERS

WildPigApocalypse

~ BOOK 1 ~

by DUNCAN McGEARY

Hamilton heard something behind him, a huffing that sounded almost like a growl. He banged his head trying to turn around.

Five javelinas surrounded him.

"Bug off!" he shouted, annoyed.

But instead of scurrying away as they usually did, they crowded closer. The one in the middle was the biggest pig he'd ever seen, with huge tusks, longer-than-normal knobby legs, and a broad chest. It had tufts of fur around its mouth and eyes.

Those eyes...

It was like looking into the eyes of something almost human: angry, malevolent, and intelligent.

The big one grunted something. A pig shot forward and ran its tusks down the side of his thigh. An agonizing pain shot through his leg and up his body, and he screamed.

He tried to get up, but his legs weren't working. The pigs watched him now, as if curious. Especially the leader. It cocked its head to one side, an almost human gesture.

Then it approached him, snorting mucus into his eyes. It stank.

When Hamilton opened his eyes again, the pig had its teeth near his throat, as if waiting for Hamilton to look. As soon as he did, it lunged and bit into the soft flesh below his chin.

Hamilton tried to scream, but it came out muffled.

He reached up and grabbed the door handle. He used it to pull himself up, and the giant pig let go of him. Hamilton felt blood flowing down his chest. His legs wouldn't support him that well, but he managed to open the door and crawl onto the seat.

It was only then that he realized that the passenger window was open.

A pig leaped through it and onto the seat.

For Bets and Sue, who as kids, read the same books as me. Misty and Stormy in the winter, Tolkien in the fall, Agatha Christie in the spring.

Chapter One

"Hamilton?" The dispatcher, Lara, couldn't quite hide her needling tone. "Guess who just called about the javelinas?"

Shit, Hamilton thought. *The guy just can't let it go.*

"I've got things to do, Lara," he said, trying to keep the irritation out of his voice. He wouldn't give the dispatcher the satisfaction. The phone was on the passenger seat on speaker. "I'll get there later this afternoon."

"He sounded pretty desperate," Lara said.

"He always does."

Actually, Hamilton's morning was clear. He just wasn't looking forward to listening to Barry Hunter bitching about the damn pigs again.

Still, without consciously making the decision, he started driving the Animal Control van toward the foothills. It was going to be a hot day. Despite the annoyance, it might be better to take care of the problem in the cool of the morning.

Barry was standing in the doorway of the porch as if expecting him. Hamilton got out and trudged up the steps, waiting for the onslaught.

Barry was uncharacteristically quiet, waiting until Hamilton reached his side. "The javelinas are getting dangerous, Hamilton," he said.

"Just stay out of their way," Hamilton began his usual reassurances. "You leave them alone, they'll leave you alone."

"Jesus, Hamilton. You don't have a clue, do you?"

"What are you talking about?"

"Dogs and cats are disappearing all over the neighborhood."

"Coyotes," Hamilton said. "Keep your animals inside if you want them to be safe—or in pens."

"That's just it," Barry said, sounding exasperated. "They're getting into the pens. Hell, they're getting into porches and houses!"

"What?" Hamilton asked dryly. "Are they using their keys?"

"Laugh if you want, buddy," Barry said. "It's happening, and you're going to have to deal with it sooner or later. Come here; I want you to see this..."

He led Hamilton to the backyard. It looked like a tornado had touched down. A row of bird feeders was knocked over, a concrete birdbath was on its side, the flowerbeds were completely overturned, and petals littered the torn-up lawn.

"Why the hell did they do this?" Barry asked. "They didn't even stop long enough to eat anything this time."

"Have you thought of a fence?" Hamilton said. His suggestion was a standard one, but he had to admit Barry had a point. No one should have to put up with this.

"How tall would it have to be?"

"To keep the deer out too? About six feet ought to do it."

"Great, just great. That's why I moved down here...to look at the back of a fence."

Hamilton was silent. There was nothing he could really do. He was allowed to kill a certain number of the wild pigs per year, no more. Personally, though, he thought that gardening was probably a nonstarter in these parts.

You want a lawn? he wanted to say. *Move to Albuquerque.* But he kept quiet. His big mouth had gotten him in trouble more than once. Probably why he was still on duty roaming the foothills instead of safely back at the air-conditioned headquarters.

Barry wasn't done. "I'm telling you, Hamilton. There is something weird going on. These fucking pigs are too damn smart. And they fucking eat everything. And what they don't eat, they fucking destroy for no good reason."

"I don't think it's *that* bad," Hamilton said. "But I'll make a report."

"Make a report," Barry repeated, eyeing him dolefully. "Yeah, you do that."

Hamilton intended to drive back to town and get some lunch in an air-conditioned diner. Instead, he found himself driving farther up into the foothills. Below was the hot, central part of the lower valley. People there had the most vermin but complained the least, and when they did complain, they had the least clout. Hamilton was rarely asked to go down to the poorer districts.

He drove past the neighborhoods of snowbird retirees. Some of these clueless folks thought the wildlife was just wonderful, deserving to be fed and pampered. They filled their Facebook pages with pictures of deer and raccoons and gushed about how amazing it was to live in nature.

Then there were those, like Barry Hunter, who were convinced the animals were pests that ought to be exterminated.

Neither camp was right as far as Hamilton was concerned.

His usual rant was coming, and he let it spill out into the empty van and out the open window: what he wanted to say to his bosses, to the public, to anyone who would listen.

"Wild animals should be wild," he said to his imaginary audience. "Don't feed the damn things. You aren't doing them any favors. You're just acclimating them to humans so they hang around, making them easier to hunt, and getting them used to human food, so they don't get the natural diet that keeps them healthy. It makes them dependent; that congregates them in overpopulated and disease-ridden vectors and makes them vulnerable to cars and trucks and generally makes the whole situation unnatural and unhealthy.

"Dammit!" he ended lamely.

He couldn't work up much outrage anymore. It was an insoluble problem as far as he was concerned. Unless they made him King of Arizona—as they should—it was only going to get worse.

He drove out of Barry Hunter's secluded neighborhood and up into the foothills to an abandoned subdivision. Here, there were paved roads and sidewalks that led nowhere and an occasional forlorn house, already weathered by neglect after only a few years.

He stopped at his favorite spot and got out of the van. He

could see the whole valley from here. It was a typically hot day, and heat currents wavered over the subdivisions. There was a slight breeze up here, its cooling effect cancelled by a brutal sun. Hamilton had long ago resigned himself to sweat and grime, so he stood in the shade of the van and took in the air.

He saw the streaking shadow from the corner of his eye. Whatever creature it was, it had gone under the car.

Hamilton sighed. He'd had this problem before. A cat had tried to hide in the shade of his car a few months ago, and when he'd driven away, he'd squashed the damn thing. Nowadays, he tried to shoo the creatures away, even the snakes, though snakes gave him the willies. That was something he kept to himself. Animal Control officers were supposed to be fearless when it came to, well, animals.

He opened up the back of the van and grabbed the snagger. He loosened the metal loop to the size he thought matched the size of the shadow he'd glimpsed and then took the end of the tube in hand. He got down on his knees and stuck his head under the van. Usually, the animals crouched near the illusory safety of the tires. He looked at the front end first, then the back.

He heard something behind him, a huffing that sounded almost like a growl. He banged his head trying to turn around.

Five javelinas surrounded him.

"Bug off!" he shouted, annoyed.

But instead of scurrying away as they usually did, they crowded closer.

The one in the middle was the biggest pig he'd ever seen, the size of a Rottweiler or bigger. Lying on the ground as he was, it appeared enormous with huge tusks, longer-than-normal knobby legs, and a broad chest. It had tufts of fur around its mouth and eyes.

Those eyes…

He was transfixed by the look he saw in them. It was like looking into the eyes of something almost human: an angry, malevolent, and very intelligent creature.

The big one, who was presumably the leader, grunted something. The pig on Hamilton's left shot forward and ran its tusks down the side of his thigh. At first, he didn't feel anything.

Then an agonizing pain shot through his leg and up his body, and he screamed. He could see the cloth of his overalls flopping onto the road and red blood squirting out over the asphalt.

Then the pig on the right did the same to his right thigh.

Again, he screamed, and he tried to get up, but his legs weren't working. The pigs were watching him now, as if curious, like children watching an anthill they'd tossed a match into.

Especially the leader. It cocked its head to one side, an almost human gesture.

Then it approached him.

It stank. The javelinas really reeked, and the odor lingered on his overalls for the rest of the day whenever he caught one. He preferred to skip the skunk pig calls whenever possible though that damned Barry Hunter always insisted on it being him answering the call.

The leader came right up to Hamilton and snorted mucus into his eyes. Hamilton closed his eyes, which were stinging and watering, and then opened them to see that the pig had its teeth near his throat. It was just waiting for Hamilton to look; as soon as he did, it lunged and bit into the soft flesh below his chin.

Hamilton tried to scream, but it came out muffled.

He reached up and grabbed the door handle. He used it to pull himself up, and the giant pig let go of him. Hamilton felt blood flowing down his chest. His legs wouldn't support him that well, but he managed to open the door and crawl onto the seat.

Just as he began to close the door behind him, he saw more javelinas coming. Five of the pigs acting so weird had been alarming. A couple of dozen of them looked like an invading army.

He started the van and put his foot down on the clutch to put it in first gear, but it was as if his leg was rubber; it simply bent under the pressure. The van ground into gear, but Hamilton knew he wasn't going to be able to do that again. Worse, the van was pointed uphill, and as he tried to put his other foot on the accelerator, the same thing happened—his leg seemed to bend, and he realized that the pigs had cut his hamstrings. The pain was so great that he screamed before he knew he would scream, and then he kept screaming.

The van stopped going forward, and he turned the wheel desperately to try to get it rolling downhill, but instead, the engine stalled, and the van started rolling backward. It was only then that he realized that the passenger window was open.

A pig leaped through it and onto the seat.

It lurched forward, and Hamilton saw a curved tusk heading for his throat, and then, there was a spray of red liquid on the inside of the front windshield.

A strange lassitude came over him as another pig jumped through the window, clamped its jaws onto his cheek, and pulled a chunk of skin away.

The driver's side door opened.

That's not possible, Hamilton thought.

Something had grabbed hold of his trousers, and he was being pulled out the door. He tumbled to the asphalt, landing on his shoulder with a loud snap. His head ground along the pavement as something pulled him first one way then another; he was surrounded by the javelinas, which were tearing parts of him away.

The pain was distant now. Once again, the giant pig came toward him. Its huge jaws opened and closed around his face, and he felt the pressure building and then heard a squishing sound as his face was torn away.

I give up, Hamilton thought.

Fucking javelinas.

Chapter Two

After Hamilton left, Barry put the lawn fixtures back together as best he could. He'd left them upended all morning because he'd wanted Hamilton to see the full extent of the damage. It felt good to put everything back in place even if he had to prop up the bird feeder posts with rocks and even if he wrenched his back getting the concrete birdbath upright.

He eased into his favorite chair—a nice, padded chair under the eaves. He poured himself a drink, closed his eyes, and basked in the heat for a while.

When he opened his eyes, they alighted on the sign he'd hung from the patio roof only a couple of days before: "The Hunter Hacienda." A guy in a booth at the weekend festival downtown had burned the letters into the wood with an old-fashioned magnifying glass.

The smell of charred wood had brought back memories of summer camp: the making of leather lanyards and signs and other folksy things. The artisan had done it in a matter of minutes with a practiced ease that had made Barry want to take up some kind of handicraft in his dufferhood.

Barry was content with a small house, someone else mowing the lawn, a pool nearby to cool off in with a little noodling, a clubhouse to play cards or billiards at, and a pickleball court. He and his wife didn't have any kids to Jenny's sorrow, and once in a while, if he was honest with himself, to his own regret as well.

He had decided to fully embrace his dufferhood.

His wife, Jenny, she was the social one. Always had been. Without her, he'd be one of those grumpy old guys you see floating around who don't participate in any activities. She was his intrepid scout, finding compatible couples to test-socialize with, and they had developed a regular group that got together every week to talk politics.

They might reside in Red State Arizona, but the people in their group were mostly good old-fashioned liberals. No doubt other groups were meeting on other patios and were full of new-fashioned idiotic conservatives, but again, Barry didn't give a damn.

Every afternoon, he'd sit on the back patio and drink vodka gimlets and wonder how he got so lucky. Jenny joined him about half the time, but she'd developed her own circle of friends. He didn't mind. He liked being alone. Always had.

He got all the socializing he wanted on Facebook, keeping up with the people back in the town he'd spent his entire career in, which was way too cold and trendy for his taste. He couldn't seem to completely let go of the Facebook thing. Spent way too much time on it.

But there was no reason to worry about it. His was an ideal existence as far as he was concerned.

Except for the damn javelinas.

Who'd have thought he'd spend his retirement at war with pigs?

"They aren't pigs," he could hear Officer Hamilton saying. "They are peccaries, an entirely different family."

"Look like pigs to me," he'd say, teasing the Animal Control officer.

"Well, they are in the same suborder as pigs. But different animals."

"Grunts like a pig, smells like a pig, it's a pig."

Hamilton would give up, shrugging.

The brush at the edge of the lawn stirred, and five large javelinas burst into Barry's backyard. The pigs looked as if they were spoiling for a fight. Some instinct made him stand up and edge for the door. He slid the door halfway closed and stood there watching them.

Their leader came forward by itself. It didn't take its eyes off Barry. It was a casual yet threatening approach. When it was ten feet away, Barry closed the door until only his head was poking out.

There had been clouds covering the sun when the javelinas had first trotted into view. Now the sun came out, and Barry could see the light glancing off the pig's eyes.

He winced, and a cold chill came over him.

Then it started clashing its teeth. Barry had heard this sound before as the herds of javelinas rooted about, knocking their tusks together.

"Keeps their tusks sharp," he could hear Hamilton's voice say. "Nothing to be alarmed about."

Well, he was alarmed. Scared, actually.

This javelina was huge. Barry was close enough to the animal to see that its tusks curved slightly, which was unusual: most javelinas have straight tusks. This pig looked more like a wild boar, a razorback.

The pig was examining him, measuring the distance, as if trying to figure out if it could get to Barry before he could close the door.

Something compelled Barry to start sliding it the rest of the way shut.

The pig shot forward so fast it was just a blur of motion. It stuck its snout through the last four inches of the opening, and it pushed the door open another inch before Barry could start countering its frantic efforts. It huffed, almost growled, and again, its yellow eyes transfixed Barry. A murderous rage and a cunning intelligence radiated from the creature. Its stink filled the house.

"Scent glands," Hamilton explained. "It's how they mark their territory. They rub it on each other, too, which is why they stink."

Some primitive primate instinct took over Barry. He roared out a strange, warlike cry that he didn't realize he had in him and kicked the creature's snout with the bottom of his slipper. He felt its tusks cut into the soft sole, and there was a flash of pain, but the javelina pulled away, and he slammed the door all the way shut and locked it for good measure.

For a few moments, the two of them stared at each other.

Barry understood. This was to be a fight to the death.

Just then, he heard his wife pulling up in the front driveway. The javelina heard it too and turned and ran back to its fellows. The animals seemed to converse, and then they ran around the corner and out of sight.

Barry turned and sprinted for the front door. His injured foot stung with every step, but he ignored the pain. He slid the last few feet to the door, slamming into it, and threw it open. His wife was halfway between the car and the door, cradling paper shopping bags in each arm.

"Hurry!" Barry shouted. "Get inside!"

To her credit, she picked up the pace. Barry could see her forming a question.

"No time!" he shouted. "Run!"

He saw a flash of motion from the left side of the house, and the five javelinas came running around the corner, moving as a solid wave.

Jenny saw them coming. She dropped the bags and sprang into the hallway. Barry slammed the door shut just as something struck the outside of it with a loud thump.

There was a narrow window running down the length of the door, and he peered out. Four of the pigs were rooting through the dropped groceries, but the big one was right there, staring back from mere inches away. It shook itself all over as if saying, "Just about got you, sucker."

Then it slowly, almost majestically, turned around and walked toward the other pigs, who moved aside and let it pick the choicest bits of food.

And then Barry's ladylike wife, who never swore, said, "What the fuck just happened?"

Chapter Three

Jenny brushed past Barry, a look of annoyance on her face that said, "It's all your fault."

She slipped on the bloody footprints he'd left on the tiles. Barry caught her just in time, stabilizing her against the wall. *Nice and cozy.* He looked into her eyes, expecting a welcoming look, he guessed. Maybe even a quick kiss. How long since they'd hugged just for the hell of it?

She pushed him away. It was subtle, but there was no doubt it was a rejection.

Then he saw the reason for her clumsiness. She was wearing high heels, what she used to call her "fuck-me shoes."

Why was she wearing them?

"You know we're retired, right?" Barry said jokingly. "You don't have to wear high heels anymore?"

A strange expression came over Jenny's face, and she glanced away. "Just because we're retired doesn't mean we have to let ourselves go." She looked back at Barry, not at his face but at his belly, which he immediately sucked in. He'd gotten on the scales that morning and discovered that for the first time in his life, he topped 200 pounds.

Now that he was paying attention, he noticed that Jenny was wearing her nicest outfit, her powder blue pantsuit and pearl necklace, and her nails and hair looked freshly done. Barry realized he had no idea where she'd spent the morning. Where had she been, anyway? She had her own friends, an almost separate life, and that was okay. It had always been just fine up in Bend, Oregon, where they'd lived for the past thirty years. She had all her work friends to go do things with while he stayed home mostly, doing promotional writing. He'd been itching to get out of that overly touristy city—which had been a nice, cozy little town when they'd first moved there—for years. But they'd had to wait until Jenny retired and got her full pension.

She hadn't really wanted to move to Arizona. She'd wanted to go back to Philadelphia, where most of her family lived. But Barry had had enough of cold climates. Until now, he'd thought she was as okay with it as he was.

"Where were you today?" he asked as if casually interested.

She ignored his question. "Why did you yell at me like that? They were just javelinas. You had me all freaked out. You made me overreact, drop the groceries."

"Jesus, Jenny!" he exclaimed. "Didn't you see them? They were out for blood!"

She looked down at his bleeding foot and frowned. "How did that happen?"

"I kicked a pig away from the door. It was trying to get in."

"Trying to get in," she repeated slowly as if he'd said Martians had landed in the backyard.

"I caught my foot on its tusk."

"Yeah, that happens when you kick a pig in the face," Jenny said dryly. She walked away from him, shaking her head. She went to the liquor cabinet and poured herself a glass of red wine. "As soon as I cool down, I'm going out and getting those groceries. And if those javelinas come near me, I'll throw a can of beans at them."

"You can't do that, Jenny. They're dangerous."

She took a sip of wine, examining him. He was getting the fish eye, the skeptical look she gave him when she thought he was being silly. "I'll be sure to watch out for the man-eating pigs."

"I'm serious, Jenny. These animals aren't acting normal. They've got rabies or something." Barry thought it was something worse than that, that these were mutant pigs, hybrids or something. But the rabies suggestion would at least sound realistic to Jenny.

"I'm going to call Hamilton," he said. He went over to the wall phone and picked up the receiver. He was already dialing, recognizing as he did so that he had Hamilton's number memorized and that that probably wasn't a good thing, before he realized there was no dial tone, which meant their Internet was probably down too since they got that service through the same company.

He slammed the phone down. "Let me borrow your cellphone."

"Where's yours?"

Barry flushed. He'd lost it weeks ago; he wasn't even sure where or when. He never used the damn thing anyway. The only reason he had it was because Jenny had bought it for him. "I can't find it," he admitted.

Jenny rolled her eyes. Then a look of puzzlement came over her face. "I…I just remembered," she said. "I put my purse in one of the bags so I could carry everything in. It's outside. I'll go get it." She started walking to the hallway.

"Don't, Jenny!" Barry exclaimed.

She kept going.

"Jenny, just don't!" Barry was shouting now. "I mean it!"

"You're being ridiculous," she said as she opened the door. She was on the top step before he could stop her.

Barry ran after her, the pain in his foot stabbing him with every step. He reached for Jenny as she reached the bottom step, only a few feet from the burst grocery bags. The food was spread out all over the concrete walk. Cans had rolled to the edge of the lawn and up against the garden. Eggshells and breadcrumbs and torn-up boxes of cereal were strewn about. The pigs had pretty much consumed everything they could get at.

There, in the middle of baking egg yolk, was Jenny's little black garnet-studded purse. Her dress purse, Barry realized, wondering again why she was so gussied up. He ignored the sinking feeling in his stomach; rather, the fear he was feeling overwhelmed it.

"Hurry," he hissed.

"Oh, hush. Pick up the groceries." She started to bend over then froze.

Coming around the corner of the house was a javelina, running at full speed. There was no mistaking its intent.

Barry had a can of food in his hand. Jenny's suggestion of throwing a can at the pigs had somehow penetrated, and he'd picked one up almost without realizing it. He threw it at the javelina as hard as he could.

He'd always been terrible at baseball (at all sports, for that matter), but some divine providence guided his hand, and the can hit the pig right on the snout. It tumbled to one side, slamming up against the house.

Thank God it wasn't the big one, Razorback, Barry thought. That monster probably would have shrugged off the strike and kept coming.

Jenny was already past him, running for the door. The pig was still rolling in the garden dirt, trying to get to its feet. Around the corner came the other four animals, led by Razorback. Then, as if that wasn't alarming enough, another half-dozen javelinas followed.

Barry staggered up the steps, feeling as if he was moving in slow motion, like in one of those dreams where his legs just wouldn't work. His wife's hand reached out of the doorway, grabbed him, and wrenched him inside. He stumbled in and fell as the door slammed shut behind him.

Barry expected a thud as the pigs hit the door. There was silence for a moment then a high, screeching sound as something sharp scraped against the wooden surface of the door and into the metal beneath.

Jenny was standing over him. Her expression wasn't one of fear, which he'd expected. Instead, she was glaring at him in profound disgust.

"Whatever did you do to make them so angry?" she asked.

Chapter Four

L yle Pederson examined the pig-sized hole in the side of his barn. The critters were getting bolder and more aggressive with every day. And there were more of them.

When he was growing up in this valley, weeks and months could go by without him seeing a javelina. They had stayed higher up in those days, rooting around in the foothills, where there was more forage.

Humans had brought the javelinas down to the valley floor. Unprotected garbage. Gardens with plump, green shoots and tasty flowers. Fewer predators. The population had exploded. He'd been warning Hamilton about the problem for years, but he could tell the Animal Control officer thought he was just an old crank.

Pederson didn't think he was a crank, but he had to admit he probably looked like one; he was old and scrawny, missing a few teeth, and had tobacco chaw in his cheek most of the time. He sported wild but sparse white hair and an unshaven chin.

He also had a Master's Degree in Engineering from Stanford and had spent a couple of decades in Silicon Valley, but he was too proud to advertise his bona fides.

He'd set about documenting the numbers of skunk pigs. He'd built an observation tower on top of his barn, bought a telescope, and started counting. And what he'd found had amazed him. The pigs moved around almost as if they knew where Hamilton was going to be next. They'd be sparse when he was around, and the minute he left an area, they'd flood back in. Then Pederson noticed that each of the packs had a leader; but most intriguingly, they all seemed to report to one giant pig, whom Pederson thought of as *the* Leader.

He took a deep breath and crawled through the pig-sized hole in the side of his barn. He found himself in the small area behind the hay bales, which was there to keep the heat from building and possibly igniting the walls. The floor was covered in pig shit, and it looked like the javelinas were spending part of their day there.

Pederson sighed and crawled back out. He had laid in a pile of lumber at back of the barn and, over the past few weeks, he'd begun reinforcing the flimsier portions of the barn. He grabbed a couple of two-by-fours and a hammer and nails and boarded up the hole. He stepped back, then decided to cover the entire side of the barn in two-by-fours, up to about five feet.

He'd have to go to town and get more wood.

He was the lumber supply store's best customer. What almost no one knew was that his little foray into Silicon Valley had made him rich. Filthy rich. He was tempted a few times to go and flash his wealth at a few county officials and get Hamilton replaced by someone a little more savvy.

But that was against his principles. Pederson lived by a code, and using money to get his way was against his code. Besides, Hamilton was a good man. It was just that the pigs were outsmarting him.

When Pederson had reinforced the barn as best he could with the available lumber, he got up and went over to the wide doors at the front of the barn. The javelinas knew about Pederson and so far hadn't dared a frontal approach. Next to the door was a shotgun loaded with buckshot. The pigs weren't the only ones keeping track of Hamilton's comings and goings. Pederson wasn't shy about using the shotgun whenever he saw a javelina on his property if the Animal Control officer was in another part of the valley.

It would make him a pariah among the retirees if they knew. Hell, some of them were so stupid, they were actually feeding the pigs. But Pederson didn't really care what the newcomers thought. He wasn't one of them. He was the last of the old-timers. As far as he knew, the only family who had resided in the valley longer than the Pedersons was the Morales family, who had been there for hundreds of years. All the rest of the pioneer families had sold out and moved away up north, where it was green—the opposite of snowbirds.

He went over to the ham radio set on the small desk near the entrance. He could've emailed his friends Emerson, Johnson, and Hawkins, but they all preferred keeping in touch via ham radio—if nothing else, just to keep in practice.

He hadn't been able to raise Emerson for more than a day, which was unusual since Emerson was wheelchairbound and didn't go far from the house. He tried again—still nothing. Even more alarming, Johnson wasn't answering either.

Before they'd signed off last time, they had reported some disturbing things.

There was a spiral staircase near the center of the barn. It had cost a fortune to buy, to have shipped to the farm, and to install. Pederson climbed the staircase, taking pleasure in its beauty, and emerged in his observation tower.

From there, he could see most of the valley.

Back in his childhood, this valley had been mostly empty. His parents' farm was situated in a prime location: near the creek with the fewest rocky pastures.

But the developers of the subdivisions that had popped up in his absence didn't care about any of that. They simply bulldozed over the boulders and piped in the water they needed. As long as there were views of the mountains, they didn't care about the practicalities that generations of farmers had had to take into account.

Pederson's dad had sold about half the ranch to these developers, making Pederson even richer than he was before, which was already way too rich to ever spend all his money.

Most of the old-timers were upset by the newcomers, the snowbirds, the retirees from up north and back east. They wanted the subdivisions stopped. But Pederson had judged that the onslaught was coming, was unstoppable, and when one of the developers had proposed a subdivision with three-acre lots, he'd been all for it because the alternative was one of those types of developments where they packed the houses in.

Then, later, he'd fought to keep the lots large even if it was environmentally dubious. He figured he'd earned the right to maintain his privacy. When the housing bubble had collapsed, he'd decided, *No more.* Between him and the Morales family, there was no more land available.

But people kept coming to the next county over, where they piled one subdivision on top of another.

The consequence was that any wildlife that couldn't adjust to the humans had been wiped out, and those animals that could adapt experienced population explosions.

Pederson scanned the foothills with his telescope, knowing all the places the javelinas spent the hot summer afternoons. The Leader was usually at one of these spots, surrounded by his followers. Lately, Pederson had noticed that the Leader had created a cadre of lieutenants, who, alarmingly, were displaying the same quantum leap in intelligence.

His offspring? Pederson wondered.

He didn't know much about biology, didn't know classifications, but he'd bet anything this was a whole new animal…species…or whatever. As such, the term javelina didn't seem appropriate any longer.

He'd begun calling them Tuskers.

He'd been meaning to contact his old friend from Stanford, Professor Samuel Marker, who was a Nobel laureate, and ask him about the possibility of such a thing happening. But he was worried Sam would think he was going senile.

No more delays, Pederson decided. It was time to contact the good professor.

I've found a whole new species of mammal, old pal, he'd say. *You can take all the credit for discovering them; all I insist is that you call them Tuskers.*

He caught movement as he scanned the hills with his spyglass and settled the scope on a pair of mountain bikers. It was the Stevensons, one of the first couples to move into the valley, who were from Washington State. Pederson had made it his business to know who all his neighbors were though most of them probably couldn't tell you who lived two houses over.

Cameron and Stacy had been busy for years building their own private bike trail, which was illegal, of course, but

Pederson kind of admired their industriousness.

The Stevensons were approaching one of the hidden hollows where the javelinas spent the days. He kept the telescope on the couple, curious to see what would happen next.

The pigs came squirting out on to the trail, catching Cameron's front tire, and he went head over heels over the handlebars. His wife crashed into his now-unoccupied bike. Once they were on the ground, the javelinas swarmed over them. Pederson thought he saw arms and legs thrashing for a short time, and then the only movement was from the pigs, who were feeding as if they were at a trough.

"Holy shit," he muttered. He reached for his phone and dialed 9-1-1.

"9-1-1; what's your emergency?"

"This is Lyle Pederson, 21 Pederson Road. I just saw a couple of mountain bikers get attacked by javelinas up on Burnt Butte."

"A cougar attack?"

"No, dammit! Skunk pigs."

"Skunk pigs?"

"*Javelinas*, you idiot!"

"Please calm down, sir. Please describe exactly what you saw."

"I saw Stacy and Cameron Stevenson bike riding. They were attacked by a group of javelinas."

"Are they hurt?"

Pederson almost hung up. He took a deep breath. "They aren't moving."

"Are you nearby?"

"No, I saw them through my telescope," Pederson said. Even as he said it, he realized what he sounded like: a crazy old coot with a telescope, spying on his neighbors. Well, it was true even if it wasn't for nefarious reasons.

"Javelinas," the operator said again as if she had never heard the term.

"Excuse me, I thought I called 9-1-1, for emergencies. I didn't think I called Nitwit Central."

"There is no call for that, sir."

"Just get someone up to Burnt Butte, about halfway up. They'll find a bike trail. Hurry."

Pederson hung up.

He went back to the telescope. The pigs had dispersed. There was no sign of the Stevensons, only the two upended bikes.

Guess it doesn't matter now, he thought.

He went down the spiral staircase and left the barn, being careful to close the big doors behind him. He got into his hulking pickup truck, his one outward luxury, and started toward town. Time to load up with as much lumber as he could find. Make the barn a fortress. He didn't know how he knew a war was brewing, but that knowledge came from the same place in his brain that had made him rich, seeing connections, seeing patterns.

He'd learned to trust those instincts.

Now, he needed to figure out how to overcome his own natural crustiness and find a believable way to warn his neighbors.

Chapter Five

Barry tried to get up, but the pain was so excruciating that he fell back with a cry. His wife's anger instantly turned to concern.

"Let me see that," she said, getting down on her hands and knees, her blue pants getting stained by the blood on the floor. She winced when she saw the gash, which ran along the middle of his foot. "We need to clean that off. Can you make it to the bathroom?"

"Sure," Barry said. He got up and hopped his way to the bathroom, putting just the slightest bit of pressure on the ball of his foot, with one hand on the wall. About halfway there, Jenny eased her shoulder under his arm and helped him make it the rest of the way.

He sat on the toilet while Jenny rooted around in the cabinet for antibacterial lotion and bandages. He watched her furrowed face. If he squinted slightly, she still looked like the twenty-year-old girl he'd met as a junior in college: a true blonde with aristocratic features and bearing, tall and thin. But he didn't need to blur his vision, for the added wrinkles only made her lovelier in his eyes.

He wondered if she was happy, if she liked living in Arizona. But even as he thought it, he realized that she'd been hinting in small ways that she didn't, in fact, like it. He'd just willfully ignored the signals.

"How about we take a long vacation to Philly?" he asked.

"Maybe later in the summer," she said after a slight hesitation. "I've got some things I need to do."

"What kind of things?" *Jesus…that sounded like the whining of a child.* "I thought that's why we came down here—so we wouldn't have things we *need* to do."

"Do you mind if we talk about it later?" she asked as she started washing the wound with a damp towel.

Barry managed not to groan from either the pain or from that strange hesitation, which he sensed meant trouble.

"What are we going to do about getting out of the house?" Jenny asked. "About letting people know?"

"Hamilton's supposed to call me later this afternoon."

She snorted. "Since when has Hamilton ever voluntarily called you, honey? I think he's on the verge of taking a restraining order out on you."

"That bad?"

"Pretty much every day."

"Oh, come on, babe. It's his job."

Jenny shook her head. "I wouldn't be counting on a call."

They fell silent. They didn't own a gun. When Barry had told Hamilton about the idea of maybe shooting a few of the pigs, or at least firing into the air to warn them off, he'd been told sternly that it was against the law to fire a gun within city limits. And to tell the truth, Barry didn't want a gun in the house. They gave him the willies.

"What if I use a bow and arrow?" he'd asked.

"Still illegal." Hamilton had been firm. "I find you are killing off the wildlife without a permit, and so help me, I'll throw your ass in jail."

"That seems so unfair!" he'd protested. "Am I supposed to just let these critters eat my garden? Destroy my lawn? Wreck all my furniture?"

Hamilton had looked as though he wanted to say something he would regret. Instead, he said, "You moved here, Barry. The wildlife was here before you. If you don't like it, then leave."

Barry had almost reported the S.O.B. over that then realized the poor guy was under a lot of stress. Barry doubted he was the only newcomer who was complaining. And much as he hated to admit it, Hamilton had a point.

So he'd tried other things. The next day, Barry had piled a bunch of stones near the patio, and when the javelinas came through, he'd started throwing missiles at them. He'd missed, mostly. But even when he hit one of them full on the flank with a loud thud, the pig had only grunted and looked at him as if to say, "That all you got, buddy?"

Barry had considered poison, but they didn't have any in the house, and he'd never gotten around to making the trip to town to buy some. Besides, he didn't want to poison all the squirrels and marmots and other innocent critters.

The thing that worked the best, at least at first, was banging on the metal lid of a garbage can. But after only a few days, the skunk pigs learned to ignore it.

And now this. "Man-eating pigs," Jenny had joked, but damned if Barry didn't wonder.

Now, he said, "The pigs can't stick around forever. They have other gardens to rape, pillage, and plunder."

Barry knew from talking to his neighbors at the pool hall that they were all having trouble with the vermin, especially his nearest neighbor, Carl Silverstein. The man was so fed up that he was building his own fence but wasn't quite done yet.

A vague plan started formulating in Barry's head. All four sides of their house had windows on the ground floor. If he ran from room to room, he could check all of them within a few seconds while Jenny kept an eye on the front. If the coast was clear, he would make a run for the car.

"Babe," he ventured.

"Yes?" Jenny recognized the tone but didn't say anything about it. For once, she seemed willing to listen to one of his schemes.

"Would you be willing to get out on the roof? Climb to the top and check out the surroundings? When the coast is clear, you can give me a signal, and I'll make a run for the car."

She looked at him as if he'd lost his mind. "Climb out on the roof?"

"Well, remember, we've done it before," he said. When they'd bought the house, they'd checked to see if it was possible to get out of the upstairs master bedroom by way of the window in case of a fire. They hadn't actually jumped off the roof but agreed that they could if they had to.

Jenny nodded. "That's not actually a bad plan. But you should be the one to get on the roof, and I should be the one to make a run for it. Seeing as how you can't run."

Barry hadn't thought of that. She was right. Problem was, he didn't think she was scared enough. She didn't really deep-down believe they were in real danger, so she wouldn't run hard enough.

But he would. Because he'd looked into Razorback's eyes.

"But we don't need to do that," she said, dismissing the plan. "Peter Gandry is coming by this afternoon to take me to dinner."

"Peter?" he said. A great dread had filled him at her words. "Out to dinner?"

A day before, he probably would have ignored it. He'd have assumed they were planning one of her benefit events. He had a vague recollection of her telling him about someone named Peter. A local real estate agent. He was also rumored to be quite the ladies' man.

"I told you about it," she said. "The neighborhood association is getting together to appeal one of the rules. You know, the one about not allowing hanging laundry outside."

"Hanging laundry." *Jesus*, he thought. *I've been blind.* His wife could care less about hanging laundry outside. Hell, Barry did the laundry in this house.

"What's going on, Jenny?" he asked.

"What do you mean?" She sounded so innocent, he knew he was onto something.

"Go ahead and tell me, babe," he urged. "Not knowing is killing me."

She stopped fussing around with putting away the first-aid supplies and cleaning the sink and turned and looked at him with a heartbreakingly serious expression. She sat on the edge of the bathtub and took Barry's hands in hers. He nearly teared up. He couldn't bear to hear what he was about to hear, but he couldn't stand not knowing either.

"I want to go back to work," she said.

"What?"

"Peter has offered me a job as a real estate agent. I've already passed the exams and everything."

Relief and confusion washed over Barry. He was having a hard time processing what she was telling him. All he knew was that Jenny hadn't told him she was having an affair.

"Did you think I was seeing someone?" she cried. She leaned forward and put her arms around him. "I'd never do that, honey. I love you so much."

He did tear up at that but managed to wipe his eyes before she let go of him and could see. "I uh…I thought we wanted to just relax down here?" he stuttered.

"So did I at first. But, honey, I'm bored out of my skull."

Barry laughed. He should have known. He was the one who had always been home, always on his own. She'd always worked in places surrounded by people. Retirement really wasn't that much of a change for him, but for her…

"I understand," he said.

"I can work as little or as much as I want," she said quickly, rushing her words as if she had thought it all out and had rehearsed the explanation. "I'll have flexible hours. We won't have to stop anything we're doing…or not doing."

He laughed again. "I get it. Sure. If it will keep you happy, I'm all for it."

She lightened up at that and sprang up. "I've got to call Peter, tell him the news… Oh."

Yeah, that brought them down to Earth again. The pigs had her phone. But suddenly, that seemed like a minor problem to Barry. Why had he been so worried about it before? It was only a bunch of pigs. *Fuck them.*

"When is Peter coming by?" he asked.

Jenny reached into her pockets, looking for her phone to check the time then stopped, flustered.

"Good thing I'm such a primitive that I still wear a watch," he said. "It's three-thirty."

"So he'll be by around fiveish, I think he said."

They got up. Barry wasn't sure what they intended to do for the next hour and a half. He knew what he *wanted* to do for the next hour and half…but it was not to be.

The entire house shook, and they both nearly lost their footing. Barry caught Jenny before she fell backward into the bathtub.

"What the fuck was that?" she asked, swearing for the second time that day, a new world record.

They ran to the living room and looked out the big picture window. Just on the horizon were their nearest neighbors, the Silversteins. They could just see the roof of the house.

Only they couldn't. Not any longer. Instead of a roof, there was a fireball and smoke billowing high into the air.

Chapter Six

Barbara Weiss clicked down the sidewalk to the Olive Garden. Her high heels were killing her. She tried to remember if she had ever worn high heels in all her working years and couldn't think of a single time. She'd been a sensible woman.

No more. Now, it was all feminine, all the time: pastel colors, dresses instead of pants, high heels, plenty of makeup. She would never look like the profile picture on her dating site, an untouched but flukey-good shot of her during her slim phase, but she was doing her best.

This was her fourth date, and she hoped that this one wouldn't be cut short. Each time she'd walked into the restaurant, the hopeful look on her date's face had dropped, and a polite veneer had taken its place. Two out of three of the men had been polite enough to at least see the meal through. One of them had gotten an "emergency" phone call within minutes and, adding insult to injury, had stuck her with the bill.

That was all right. Barbara could afford it. She had generous pensions, double dipping from both the county and the state. Besides, she was beginning to think she should offer to pay for at least half the meal anyway. It was not the way she remembered dating, but apparently, it was the new way of doing things.

This time, it was her turn to recoil. The man was fat, nothing like his profile. That would have been all right, but when he gave her a hug, he stunk, a not-bathing kind of stink, something that he could do something about if he cared. If he stunk on a first date, she could only imagine how he'd smell the rest of the time.

Barbara stuck it out. He was actually fairly interesting, but she got the distinct impression that he was a hoarder from his description of all his flea market purchases. She let him peck her on the cheek and hurried away without a commitment to a second date.

That's it, she thought. *Four strikes, and I'm out.*

She'd never much liked the idea, but so many of her Facebook friends had told her about their luck with Internet dating that she'd felt she had to give it a try.

Moving down to Arizona was looking like a mistake. Oh, she loved her house. She loved the views. She liked the town and the people. But she hated the fact that old women far outnumbered old men. She'd never been able to compete in the dating game.

Barbara had always been stocky. Not fat but solid, "built like a linebacker," her dad had said fondly, not knowing how much it hurt. She'd met Howard at the senior prom. He was with a girl who got drunk and belligerent, and Barbara, in her take-charge way, had taken the girl aside and talked her down.

While she was doing that, her own date wandered off to join his friends, none of whom she knew, and she found herself standing there talking to Howard. They'd hit it off from the start. He was tall and strong, and sure, maybe he had an ugly mug, but he was kind and patient, and he loved her.

They'd had two children, both of whom had gone on to higher education and lived back east.

She'd had the best of it. Her career, her marriage, her family, her friends.

Then, five years ago, Howard had died, most of her friends had wandered off or passed away, and she was forced into mandatory retirement by state and county regulations. She'd rattled around the big house for a few years, hoping for an occasional visit from Jeremy and Sarah. Instead, her kids had invited her to move back East, to be closer to her grandchildren.

Barbara had finally decided she needed to get her life going again. She needed a change.

So she moved to Arizona.

She walked out of the Olive Garden, and the blast of heat almost melted her on the spot. Her makeup seemed to be drying into a solid mask on her face. She wanted to cry, but she raised her chin and marched to her car. She couldn't remember the last time she had cried. One long cry when Howard died, and before that...never?

She tore off her high heels and gripped the steering wheel.

She drove home slowly, taking the long route, unwilling to sit in her big living room by herself, watching TV or reading a book.

Alone.

After meandering about, driving down roads she'd never driven down before, she pulled into her driveway and pushed the button on the garage door opener. She didn't pull in right away but sat there idling, thinking about nothing. She glanced at her front yard. She'd decided when she'd moved there not to put in a lawn or a garden, conscious of how much water it would waste.

She smiled to herself. Her old coworkers would have laughed at the idea of her being an environmentalist, but Barbara had always been a secret liberal despite her occupation. In fact, the only social activity she enjoyed down here in Arizona was with the group of other liberals she'd found, who had afternoon barbecues and patio parties once a week. They called themselves the Bleeding Hearts Club: Jenny and Barry Hunter, Stacy and Cameron Stevenson, the Silversteins, the Fosters, and old Billy Patterson, who'd been making eyes at her but was so ancient that she hadn't seriously considered him.

Maybe it's time to reconsider, she thought. *I think I just need a companion, and I'm not going to be particularly picky about him.*

Except...he can't stink.

She pulled into the driveway, got out, and walked around the front of the car to get to the door to the house. She passed briefly into the sunlight and saw three pigs approaching.

Ordinarily, she'd have ignored them. She'd heard that her neighbors were having trouble with the javelinas, especially Barry Hunter, who brought the subject up at nearly every meeting of the Bleeding Hearts Club. But because she didn't have any plants to attract the critters, she hadn't seen them much.

They were a new species to her. Central Oregon didn't have them. They kind of fascinated her in their boldness.

These three were being especially bold. They were getting closer and closer. She looked into the eyes of the leading pig.

Barbara didn't hesitate. She reached into her purse, pulled out her Glock, and started firing. Her first three bullets each hit one of the pigs square in the head, but she emptied the clip as she was trained to do, grabbed the second clip, and reloaded. She held the gun out, looking for movement.

Then Barbara Weiss, sheriff of Crook County in Central Oregon for more than twenty years, turned and opened the door to her house.

Chapter Seven

Hooking up the trailer with the motocross bike to his SUV reminded Peter Gandry how much financial trouble he was in. He owed money on the car, the bike, hell, even the trailer.

But the bike was the only thing that kept his fourteen-year-old son interested in hanging out with him, so he would do just about anything to keep it from being repossessed. That would be too humiliating and the last straw with Josiah, who already blamed him for the divorce.

Peter had two more meetings that day, and then he could head for Phoenix to spend a few days with his son. Besides, hauling the motorcycle around would look wholesome to the clients, like he was an outdoorsy kind of guy and a good father.

Morales was waiting for him in Lucille's Diner at the back table, already eating his breakfast. Peter decided to overlook the insult since he couldn't afford breakfast anyway. He was getting that desperate. The last sale he'd made had been to the dyke sheriff from Oregon. He was just thankful he hadn't had to fuck her.

"Just coffee," he said to Mary, the waitress. He gave the cute girl his best smile.

He knew his most valuable sales attributes were his full head of black hair, his dark brown eyes and long eyelashes, and his long, lanky cowboy body. He covered his one weakness, a slightly receding chin, with a dark beard, left long in the all the right places.

None of his charm worked on Morales, who was a hard case. The Mex (he used to think "spic," but that had gotten him in big trouble with his Chamber of Commerce buddies when he'd let it slip into a joke once) drove a beat-up old pickup and lived in a beat-up old house, so Peter figured he needed the money. But despite owning acres of prime land, he wouldn't sell a single inch no matter how much Peter offered.

He had a Hail Mary, last-ditch plan. He'd noticed how Morales' eyes strayed to and followed the shapely bodies of tall blondes. In fact, he'd seen the Mex practically drool at the sight of Jenny Hunter, one of the newcomers to town. It so happened that the woman had inquired about a position in the Gandry Real Estate Company, and he almost had her aboard. Now, he wouldn't mind fucking Jenny even if she was twenty years older than him. She didn't know it yet, but her first job would be to work on Morales.

The money he was offering wasn't his, sadly. Bart Hoskins, the banker, had extended him credit for this one project only and was keeping an eye on him so that he couldn't divert it or siphon it off for his bills.

"I have thought about your offer," Morales said with a thick accent. "I will sell you one acre of land. One acre to see what you do."

The Mex shoved the map with the plots marked on it toward Peter and pointed to a piece of land very close to the river. Peter started getting excited. He figured it was probably a piece of shit property, but it was the first time Morales had made the slightest concession.

If he couldn't sway Morales into selling a few dozen acres in the next several months, Peter was sunk. Morales was one of two original landowners in the valley who still had big enough chunks of desirable land to create a subdivision on.

Peter pulled out his checkbook with a flourish and wrote out the check right then and there. Get Morales spending a little money, give him a taste of the good life, and all things were possible.

He stood up. "You won't regret it, Flaco," he said. "Can we meet again in a week?"

Morales nodded. "Sure, sure."

"Good! I'll see you same time, same channel!" Peter turned and walked out of the diner, conveniently forgetting to pay for his coffee.

Flaco finished his meal, feeling a little bad for the real estate agent. He had no intention of selling the man any of his useful land. The plot he'd just sold was one of those awkward pieces of land that was so angled and bordered by roads and natural features that it wasn't really useful for anything.

He pocketed the check and waved at Mary. His credit was good all over town. He may not have looked like he had much money, but he always paid his bills.

He felt a little chagrined about his phony accent. When he'd first met Peter Gandry, he'd used the accent as a joke—his daughter thought it was hilarious—and then, when the real estate agent had bought into it, he'd felt as though he needed to keep it up.

Truth was, he probably spoke better English than Gandry. It killed Flaco that the people of the valley treated him like an immigrant when his family had lived there long before any of the Northerners had showed up.

He walked out to his truck and saw a javelina standing under the shade of a nearby tree. When he was growing up, he'd rarely seen the skunk pigs. When he had seen one, they were usually running away. This one was particularly big and bold. Flaco was whistling as he unlocked his pickup, but when he looked into the creature's eyes, he stopped mid-tune.

Its yellow eyes seemed to be measuring him, as if wondering if it could take him down.

Flaco crossed himself and quickly got into the truck. He probably would have forgotten all about it, but as he was pulling out of the parking lot, a pack of javelinas blocked his way. He honked, but they didn't move. He was ready to get out and shoo them away when one of them turned and looked at him. Again, it was a shock. Intelligence and malevolence radiated out of those eyes. Was it the same pig, the one from under the tree?

He looked in the rearview mirror and realized that the first pig was now only a couple of yards behind the pickup. If he had gotten out of the truck, he could have been blindsided.

He honked again then edged forward until the javelinas slowly, contemptuously, moved out of the way.

Flaco drove home, deep in thought. At the one stoplight in town, he pulled out the check. It was free money, and he wanted to do something frivolous with it.

He walked into his house, checking the surroundings first. The pigs had scared him that much.

His daughter, Alicia, lived with him along with his five-year-old grandson, Felix. His son-in-law was in Afghanistan.

"Pack your bags, daughter," he said when he found her. "I'm taking you to Hawaii."

"What?" she laughed. "It's the middle of the school week."

Alicia taught third grade at the local school.

He waved her comment off as if it was of no concern. "You've just gotten the flu. We'll be back in a week. Come on; you haven't been on a vacation since Enrique left. My treat."

"You really mean it? Felix too?"

"No, we'll leave Felix here," Flaco said with a straight face. "*Of course* I mean it! We leave first thing in the morning."

He went to his office and closed the door.

He crossed himself again as he thought of the javelinas. Those creatures hadn't been normal. They were possessed or something.

Flaco thought something bad was about to happen to this town, and he wanted to be gone when it happened.

Besides, he'd always wanted to try surfing.

Peter Gandry had one more meeting before picking up Jenny Hunter at five o'clock. As he drove down the street in front of Lucille's Diner, he saw a group of javelinas crossing the road.

He sped up, swerved, and caught one of them on the flank, sending it flying into the air. He looked in the rearview mirror to see it land on its head and lie there, unmoving. Then he took a survey of his surroundings to make sure no one had seen what he'd done.

He hated the damn pigs. They were going to be the death of the community someday if word got out to the snowbirds about how destructive they were.

Bart Hoskins was waiting for him at Earps, the upscale restaurant in the refurbished hotel in town. The hotel was in trouble, he knew, but he'd been forced out of that deal early, which had turned out to be a lucky thing for him. *Fuck them.*

Bart had also already ordered without him, and Peter felt the same weird mix of resentment and relief.

"How's it going with Morales?" the banker said without preamble.

"Great! I bought an acre from him." Peter produced the check record and showed the banker the plot on the map.

"Useless," Bart said bluntly. "I know that plot."

"Yeah, but the money softens up Morales for the next one. Trust me, I know how it works. I've got another plan in the works too." He was thinking about the tall, sexy-for-all-her-age blonde, Jenny Hunter.

Bart just grunted.

"How's it going with Pederson?" Peter asked, changing the subject. Pederson was the other local landowner in the valley who had viable swaths of land.

"You can forget about that," Bart said, waving his fork, dismissing the subject.

"Why? The old guy must have *huge* property taxes, and he barely farms his land."

Bart put down his fork and knife and examined him. "Well…I'm not supposed to say anything, and if you repeat this, I'll deny I said it, but…Lyle Pederson could buy and sell you and me twice over and not even blink."

"Oh," Peter said, deflated. So it was down to the Mex, Flaco Morales, who showed no real enthusiasm about letting go of anything.

"Look, Peter," Bart was saying. "I've been patient about your debts because I know you're trying hard. But really, you've got to get Morales on board in the next couple of weeks or I'm going to have to close you down."

By habit, Peter almost wound up a spiel, but he kept quiet. He was just too tired. He wasn't going to make it; he could see that now. It was all going to shit.

His five o'clock meeting with Jenny Hunter was his last chance.

He slipped out of the restaurant before the bill arrived. On the way to the car, he had an idea. He pulled out his phone. It took him a couple of minutes to find the number.

"Hello, Mr. Pederson? This is Peter, from Gandry Real Estate? Listen, sir, I know you're busy, but I have some parties who are very interested in your lower acres… Hello? Mr. Pederson?"

Peter threw the phone onto the seat, and it bounced onto the floor. He didn't bother to pick it up.

Yep, it was all going to shit.

Chapter Eight

As it happened, both Jenny and Barry climbed out onto the roof. They had a small deck at the end of the second-floor hallway, which had seemed like a nice feature when they bought the house but which they never used. Unfortunately, the deck seemed to be in the path of some kind of natural wind tunnel, so it was unpleasant to sit out there for long.

But the railing was low, and they could get onto the roof from there. They climbed up to the peak of the roof on all fours, sat down gingerly, trying to gain their balance, and looked to the east.

They couldn't see anything but smoke. Not a sign of the Silverstein house. From there, they could also see Pederson's old barn, and without the smoke, they probably could have seen the Underwoods' place. They'd never met the latter couple, who were usually traveling around Europe and who kept to themselves when they were home.

"Barry…" His wife's voice was low and worried.

"We'll be okay," he said but then realized she was looking at something on the ground. A few yards from the house, there was a big hole in the side yard. Split cables were visible from where they sat.

"Well, now we know why we couldn't call out," Barry said.

Jenny nodded toward the spiral of smoke. "Do you suppose…?"

"Yeah, Carl had gas lines. He was bragging about how much money he was saving last winter. I thought he was kind of nuts since it only gets cold around here for such a short time."

"But wouldn't gas lines be metal or something?"

"Something pretty hard, I'd have to believe. But, babe, did you see the damage to the outside of our front door?"

When Barry had been making his—what had seemed to him—slow-motion escape from the pigs at the front steps, he'd seen heavy grooves in the door panels. The marks had appeared to be at least an inch deep.

"That smoke is going to bring emergency vehicles," Jenny said. "Even if no one calls them."

They stared at the smoke, contemplating it. Then both of them had the same idea.

Barry began, "We should..."

"...signal them," Jenny finished.

They slid carefully down the roof on their butts, one scoot at a time, and climbed over the railing back into the hallway.

"I'll check the kitchen," Jenny said and hurried off.

Barry limped to his den. He kept a flashlight tucked in one corner of the bookshelf near the door. He reached for it, paused for a second to pray to whatever deity would listen, and flipped the switch.

There was light, but it was dim. He shook the flashlight, and it brightened for a moment then went even dimmer. *Shit.*

Jenny was clambering up the stairs. "Found it!" she said excitedly. She had the big flashlight that they took camping. It was supposed to be heavy duty. "This ought to be strong enough."

"Do we have any extra batteries?" he asked worriedly then added, "It's still pretty bright out. I hope they can see us." By this time, they could hear sirens rapidly approaching. Barry tried to identify the alarms, wondering if there were any police officers coming. Police officers had guns.

They climbed back onto the roof. Red emergency vehicles were rushing down the long road to the Silversteins'. It looked to be a two-alarm fire. But then, two fire trucks were all the township owned. Barry thought he saw the cherry top of a cop car too.

"Do we have anything that will make noise?" he asked.

"I think I have an old coaching whistle," Jenny said. "I think it's in the junk drawer. Want me to get it?"

"Let's try signaling with the flashlight first."

"When should we do it?

The sirens had stopped, but the lights were still flashing. Overhead, the pall of smoke was getting darker as the water from the firefighters' hoses began hitting the flames.

"Let's wait a few minutes," Barry said. "They're going to be too busy to be looking anywhere else for a while."

They sat close together, and Barry put his arm around Jenny, getting more and more secure on their precarious perch. It suddenly occurred to him that he was having fun…well, maybe not fun, but it was all very exciting.

Barry didn't normally look for excitement. He'd always said that even if you try to do everything to eliminate risk, trouble will still find you, so why go looking for it? But this crisis seemed to have awakened him out of a torpor he hadn't even known he'd been in. *The situation is dangerous,* his head told him. *It's exciting,* said his heart. And his soul didn't really believe that they'd be hurt, either Jenny or him. They'd come out of it okay; they always did.

The smoke was getting really thick. When Jenny coughed, Barry took his arm from her shoulders. "I'm thinking maybe we should try now."

Jenny didn't immediately respond. "Are you sure?" she finally said. "I mean, I don't see any of the pigs around. Maybe we can get to the car and just drive away. We'll look pretty silly when we tell them we're trapped by…by javelinas."

"Yeah, well, let them deal with the beasts. I don't mind looking silly."

She laughed. "Okay. You're right. Who cares?" She lowered the flashlight and turned it on. "What's S.O.S. again?"

That brought him up short. "Three short, three long, three short…I think."

She started to flash the signals.

"Wait!" he said, suddenly panicking. "Maybe it's three long, three short, three long."

She started chuckling, but didn't stop what she was doing. "I think they'll get the message either way."

It seemed as if she was signaling for hours though it was

probably only a few minutes. Barry checked his watch. It was a quarter to four o'clock. If nothing else, they should probably save some of the battery life for when it got dark. There would probably still be firefighters around.

Of course, dark was when the javelinas really got active.

"My fingers are getting tired," Jenny said.

"Let me do it for a while," he said, reaching for the light, but at the same moment, they heard the blare of sirens.

Whoop, whoop, whoop! Beep, beep, beep! Whoop, whoop, whoop!

"I think they've seen us!" Barry shouted.

He dared to stand up, there on the steepest part of the roof, and waved his arms and hooted at the top of his voice. A vast sense of relief filled him, and he realized that he'd been more worried and frightened than he was willing to admit.

Whoop! Whoop! Blaaark… blaaark, bl…

Barry sat down abruptly. He could see what looked like a dark wave washing along the ground toward the emergency vehicles. He couldn't make sense of it. And then he heard gunshots, three or four loud cracks before they abruptly stopped.

And then, drifting from the Silverstein house, he heard screams.

Chapter Nine

"9-1-1; what is your emergency?"

"This is Barbara Weiss, 302 Bradford Court. I was just attacked by three javelinas."

There was silence on the other end of the line. Barbara had expected the operator to scoff or at least sound skeptical. She could hear whispering in the background, and when the operator came back on, she sounded businesslike.

"We are advising people to stay indoors."

Barbara hesitated at that. Had there been more than one incident?

"No problem. I took care of it," she said.

"How did you do that, ma'am?"

"I blew their brains out."

"Ma'am, it is illegal to fire your gun within the city limits."

"Don't teach your grandmother how to suck eggs," Barbara responded automatically. It was her standard phrase whenever one of her young deputies tried to act as if he or she knew more than Barbara did.

"Pardon?"

"Never mind. Listen, I was a sheriff for over twenty years and a deputy for ten years before that, and there isn't a single place in this country where the law doesn't allow for self-defense."

"I understand, ma'am. We'll be sending an officer out as soon as possible to take a report. In the meantime, we suggest that you stay indoors."

"Will d—" Barbara started to say.

"And sheriff," the operator broke in. "Keep your weapon handy."

Barbara hung up slowly. Something was going on. She recognized the tone in the 9-1-1 operator's voice. The operator was limited in what she could say, but she'd managed to convey a lot with her choice of words.

Barbara went to the living room window and opened the curtains. There, standing in what seemed to be rows, were dozens of javelinas looking back at her.

She closed the curtains, unnerved. She went to her pantry, pulled out the box of bullets, and counted them. She'd once figured it was more than enough for a lifetime even with occasional target practice. But she'd just witnessed fifty pigs looking at her as if she was dinner.

She took the box to the kitchen table and started reloading her empty clip. She was going to have to override her training and fire only as much as she needed. She'd killed her attackers with three bullets and then wasted the last twelve bullets in her clip making them deader than dead.

She got up, went to her closet, and put on some sensible clothes. They felt comfortable and right.

No more dresses. No more high heels.

The shirt had epaulets; she'd bought it because she'd liked them. They had felt appropriate. If she put a couple of patches on them, the outfit could've passed for a uniform. She pulled on her old boots and cinched her belt tight then clipped on her holster.

That's more like it, she thought. No more pretending she was a "lady"—whatever that meant. Oh, she was a woman, all right. Those men she had "dated" had no idea what they were missing.

And she could take care of herself.

She pulled out her cellphone and punched in her daughter's number. As usual, it was busy. Sarah made dolls and— unexpectedly—had become quite the Internet tycoon. When Sarah had first married Jonathan Perkins and decided to become a housewife, Barbara hadn't approved. *All that higher education going to waste,* she'd thought, but she'd known better than to say anything.

She needn't have worried. Sarah was busier at home with

her doll empire than she ever would have been working for a corporation. And richer too. Her daughter had maids and private tutors for her homeschooled kids and everything she needed. Barbara had even seen an article on her in *USA Today.*

The problem with such success was that Sarah could rarely get away. Even when Barbara visited, Sarah had little time for her despite her best efforts. There was always some emergency or another or something else going on with her business that required her attention.

The other problem was that the phone was always busy. Oh, Barbara could stay on the phone until Sarah answered, and her daughter would do her best to be pleasant, but there would be a stressed-out edge to her voice implying that she needed to get back to work.

If Sarah didn't answer, the dutiful daughter would call back later when she noticed the missed call. But the same thing would happen; she'd have that same stressed-out tone. Sometimes, Barbara didn't bother to answer the return call.

She stared at Jeremy's number for several minutes. Then she took a deep breath and tapped the number.

"Hello?" It was a little girl's voice.

"Hi, Emily! This is your grandmother."

"Who?"

Barbara felt her heart sink, but she pushed on. "Your grandmother."

"Grandma Martha?"

"No, sweetie. This is your Grandma Barbara."

"Dad!" the little girl shouted into the receiver, and Barbara had to pull the phone away from her ear.

She tried again. "Emily, how are you? Did you get the iPhone I sent?"

"Dad wouldn't let me keep it," came the little voice.

"Oh."

"Dad! It's Grandma Barbara!"

"Emily…" Barbara said, trying desperately to think of something to say to engage the little girl. She knew so little about her. Jeremy seemed almost determined to keep information about Emily away from her.

"Hello? Mom?"

Barbara braced herself. Conversations with her son were always awkward. He'd become a defense attorney and took mostly death penalty cases. He'd been raised a liberal, but he'd gone far beyond that. Barbara had once made the mistake of playing devil's advocate to what she considered his extreme views, and as a result, Jeremy actually thought she was a conservative. What else could a sheriff in the Wild West be?

Jeremy had left Prineville for college and never come back except for short, begrudging visits.

"Is something wrong?" his deep voice demanded.

"No, Jeremy. I just want to hear your voice. I was so glad to speak to Emily."

"Yeah… Listen, Mom. Can I call you back tonight? I'm in the middle of something."

"Of course, Jeremy. Call me back when you can. I'm always here."

They hung up, and she kicked herself. *"I'm always here."* *How pathetic.*

She went to the front of the house, drawing her Glock. She threw open the door. Half a dozen javelinas were rooting around in the bare dirt and rocks. She started blasting, catching three of the pigs by surprise and killing them. Two of the others were winged as they ran, and the third got away completely. As she ejected the spent clip and loaded another one with practiced ease, the unharmed javelina turned and gave her a look that almost stopped her from finishing the motion.

It was a warning look. *You've messed with the wrong pig,* the look said.

Barbara laughed, finished inserting the clip, and raised her Glock. But the javelina had disappeared around the side of the house. She thought about pursuing it but decided not to go without backup. *You* have *no backup,* came the thought.

Instead, she went back to the living room and opened the curtains. The pigs were gone.

She pulled the armchair around to face the window and sat down to wait.

Chapter Ten

"What's happening?" Jenny said. "I don't understand! What's happening?"

The smoke from the Silverstein house was expanding into a mushroom cloud.

"Let's get inside," Barry said. He got up and walked down the roof, for some reason no longer scared of falling off. He was numb. He jumped over the railing and then turned and helped his wife.

He was still favoring his right leg, but the pain didn't seem as bad. Mostly, he was just scared. All his plans—going into town, getting a gun, blasting the javelinas away, law or no law—seemed inadequate now.

Trained police officers had apparently just been taken down in seconds.

That wave he'd seen, that wasn't the original five pigs or even the dozen or so more he'd seen later. That had appeared to be hundreds of them, hundreds of pigs on the rampage. He'd need a machine gun, a flamethrower, a tank!

They had reached the kitchen when they heard a car pull up out front.

"Peter…" Jenny breathed in and gave a cry of alarm when she breathed out. She ran for the door.

"Don't open it!" Barry shouted. There was steak knife lying on the counter. He grabbed it and followed her.

She opened the door, and for a moment, Barry thought everything would be all right. Peter was getting out of his SUV. He had a small trailer on the back with a motorcycle in it, and Barry remembered something about his kid being active in motocross.

He saw something darting for his wife's legs and dove at it. He drove the knife into the javelina's side, killing it when its tusks were mere inches from Jenny's thighs.

"What the fuck?" Peter said. He was halfway up the walkway, looking at them in shock.

Fortunately, there was only one "guard" at the doorway. And even in the heat of the moment, Barry knew that it had been planted there on orders from Razorback, as crazy as that sounded.

Peter was a good-looking guy: tall, dark, and swarthy, the kind of guy that Jenny would always say was handsome when she saw them on TV. Barry wasn't that dark and not very swarthy, so he always wondered about that. In comparison with Peter, he was average height with gray, thinning hair and a beard. Even when he'd been younger, his hair had been an unremarkable light brown.

Yet at that moment, Barry knew that there was nothing to be jealous about.

"Run!" he shouted, but Peter simply stood there with his mouth open.

"Peter!" Jenny screamed. "Get inside!"

He finally started moving, but it was too late. There must have been twenty of them, swarming from either end of the SUV, but the one that got him was a smaller one that came from under the car. It shot forward, and its tusks cut into the tendons at the back of Peter's ankles, and he fell as if his legs had been cut off.

He tried to rise, but the other pigs reached him, and one of them went for his throat. Peter tried to scream, but nothing came out. Blood spurted from both sides of his neck, and his head flopped forward. Then it detached and rolled down the walkway.

Jenny was screaming, and Barry had to pull her back so that he could slam the door. The pigs were so busy feeding, it was as if they didn't even know the other humans were there.

"I realized they could hurt us," Jenny said. "I never thought they could *kill* us."

They were sitting at the kitchen table with drinks in their hands. Barry had poured them both a stiff one, pure vodka to the top of the glass, and Jenny was choking it down. Her shaking hand was becoming steadier as her words became more slurred.

Barry remembered stories of medieval kings or knights being gored to death by wild boars, and it had always seemed an ignominious and silly way to die. Now, he realized there was nothing funny about it.

But he'd never heard of pigs swarming like this. It was almost as if they were being directed with tactical planning.

Which was nuts.

"We'll stay inside until it blows over," he said. "We can't be the only ones this is happening to."

She nodded. Barry knew he'd get no more argument from her about staying inside.

It got dark, and it grew eerily quiet. They turned on the TV for a few moments, but its blaring cheerfulness was so incongruous to their situation that they quickly switched it off again.

"We've got water and a full pantry. We'll just stick it out," Barry said, suspecting he was starting to repeat himself. He always did get verbose when drunk.

Maybe not a good idea to get incapacitated, he thought. He put down the glass with a full inch of vodka still at the bottom, proud of his restraint.

"Let's go upstairs," he said. Jenny nodded, and they stood up from the table, took each other's hands, and walked up to the bedroom. She spent extra time in the bathroom, and he could hear her crying but decided she probably wanted to be alone to let it out and that she'd put up a brave front when she was with him.

After she came out, Barry went in. After he did his business, he happened to look in the mirror. He was shocked by the man who stared back at him. A thousand-yard stare is what they called it. Shell shock. His cheeks were gaunt even though he hadn't skipped a single meal, and there were dark shadows under his eyes.

He slid open a drawer and pulled out his pill bottle. He sometimes took half a Xanax to sleep. He thought about taking a couple then closed the drawer again.

He went back to the bedroom. The lights were out. Jenny wasn't moving, but he knew she wasn't asleep.

The pigs are most active at night, came the thought.

As if in response, he heard a crash from downstairs.

Chapter Eleven

Pederson was on his fourth trip back from town, loaded down with lumber. He'd cleaned the hardware store out of shotgun shells. On his third trip, there had been five other people in line. All he had to do was say the word "Javelinas?" out loud, and the conversation had taken off.

They were all having trouble with aggressive bands of pigs. Pederson knew all the names of the people in line though he doubted they knew who he was. He'd made it his business to know who his neighbors were.

"My cat went missing," Harvey Johansson said. "I keep her inside most of the time, and she's a scaredy cat. It would take some doing to catch her off guard. But…these skunk pigs, they're getting way too aggressive. And sneaky."

"I think we need to clean them out," said Jerry Olsen. "Cut their numbers down."

Fred Carter spoke up. "I came around the corner of my house to change hoses and ran smack dab into one. I swear it growled at me. Pigs don't growl, do they?"

The conversation inspired them all to load up. The entire shelf of ammunition was completely wiped out.

"Maybe we should leave some for others," Anthony Lawrence said doubtfully.

"Don't worry," the clerk said cheerfully. "We have a whole warehouse full."

But Pederson noticed, on his fourth trip, that the shelves were still empty. He stared at the high-end bow and arrow set for a long time then reluctantly turned away. He suspected he didn't have time to learn even the rudiments of bow hunting.

Though how hard could it be? he asked himself.

He turned around and snagged the bow and arrow set and took it to the counter. The box was dusty. The huge price tag meant that most people in this town could never afford it. It was a showpiece.

The same clerk was there, no longer looking so cheerful. He eyed the huge price tag on the bow and looked at Pederson doubtfully, but when he was handed a Black Card, he ran it through, and it cleared.

"What's going on, Mr. Pederson?" the clerk asked. "Everyone is acting crazy. I can't raise anyone at the warehouse. My boss hasn't come in today. Is there something I should know?"

"What's your name, son? Where you from?"

"Mark," he said. "Mark McCallister. I'm from Idaho."

"Idaho, good. Did you live in the country? Know how to handle a gun?"

"Yes, sir. Everyone knows how to handle a gun where I come from."

"Good," Pederson said. "Buy one of your fine wares and take it home along with a box of ammunition. Don't bother to come to work tomorrow. Where are you living now, Mark?"

"In town, over the old Sweeny grocery store."

"You should be safe."

"What do you mean, safe? What the hell is going on?"

"Just stay indoors. If you see any javelinas, get inside quick."

Pederson left him there with his mouth open. He didn't know the clerk, which meant he was newly arrived in town. The young man might not even know what a javelina was.

Pederson needed to get back to the farm. When he was driving into town, he'd seen a huge pack of the javelinas coming down the road. By the time he'd reached the turn in the road where they had been, they'd vanished into the underbrush. The sight had disturbed him. Before this week, he'd never seen more than twenty javelinas together.

He was headed out the door of the hardware store when he saw Bart Hoskins, the head of the local United Way chapter. He was a banker and one of the few people in town who knew about Pederson's wealth. He was rotund man, originally from

L.A., but he pretended to be one of the old-timers because he'd arrived a couple of years before most of the other snowbirds.

The banker winked at Pederson like he always did. Pederson had made it clear that if word ever got out about his money, the largesse he bestowed on the United Way would come to an end. Even then, he sometimes wondered if Bart's love of notoriety would overcome his better nature.

"Lyle, good to see you!" Hoskins boomed. Then the big man noticed the bow and arrow and looked askance at them. Hoskins was against all guns, all hunting, and anything else that might pare back the wildlife. If he had his way, all the animal species would be allowed to overpopulate and starve to death.

"Let me ask you something," Pederson said on the spur of the moment. He never could resist pulling Hoskins's chain. "Have you been having trouble with javelinas?"

A cloud passed over the banker's face, and Pederson knew he'd hit a sore spot.

"Well, they were here before us," Hoskins said. "Besides, I don't believe in wasting water on lawns and gardens, so I got nothing to complain about." There was something in his voice though…

"But?" Pederson prompted.

"They killed my cat!"

"Have you thought of getting a gun?"

"What?" The banker tried to act surprised, but Pederson saw the look of guilt in the man's face. He *had* bought a gun. Pederson would bet anything on it.

"They have as much right to exist on this land as we do," Bart said stubbornly. "Maybe more so."

"Yeah, keep telling yourself that. Meanwhile, be careful, Bart. You hear?"

The banker nodded, and they exchanged a look, man to man, and passed each other without another word.

Pederson had more wood in the back of his pickup than he probably needed, but then, he also had more money than he could ever spend. The passenger seat and the compartment behind the front seat were filled with groceries. For the first time in his life, Pederson had bought bottled water. He'd tried to think of everything.

He shoved the bow and arrow on top of the rest.

It was probably all for nothing. They'd call the state troopers in or the National Guard. A few more attacks and no one would be able to deny the problem.

But...there was that nagging feeling. He'd had it the week before the stock market crashed. He'd called his broker and told him—no, *ordered* him because he could tell the broker was going to lollygag—to sell everything.

The broker had called back a week later to thank him because Pederson had been so adamant that the broker had also sold a portion of his own portfolio.

The one thing Pederson had learned from his years in Silicon Valley was trust your own instincts even when everyone else disagreed with you; maybe especially when everyone disagreed with you.

He was probably traveling a little too fast on his way home. He knew every turn in the road, every bump. But he didn't expect to encounter a javelina standing in the middle of the road.

If he'd had even one more second to think about it, he would have run over the animal. But his natural impulses took over, and he swerved to miss the pig. His right front tire went off the right side of the road and seemed to want to jerk the pickup off the cliff. He corrected. He'd planned for this moment for years. Most people overcorrected, sending them careening to the other side of the road, either smashing head-on into oncoming traffic or continuing down the other side, usually flipping the car. So he tried to moderate his correction, but it was no use. The momentum still sent him across the road. Fortunately, the road was rarely traveled, so it was the bank on the other side that came barreling toward him. He braced himself for impact.

The last thing he remembered was the airbag coming toward his head as if in slow motion. It was impossible that he could have seen it, but he had a vision of the wood flying through the air over the pickup, the planks impaling themselves into the sandy bank.

And then darkness.

Chapter Twelve

Jenny whimpered at the sound of the crash downstairs, and Barry almost joined her. But despite the equality of their marriage—hell, she had earned most of their income over the years, but he'd never felt like less of a man because of it—he felt something old-fashioned rising in him, giving him courage: the need to protect his woman.

"Don't go out there," Jenny said as he approached the bedroom door.

"Where's the big flashlight?" he asked.

"I left it on the deck. Are the lights out too?" she asked in a steadily rising voice as if that was the most terrifying thought of all.

Barry flipped the bedroom light on and off a couple of times to reassure her. The light dazzled their eyes. "I was thinking of it more as a weapon," he said.

"Can't we just wait until morning?"

"There might still be something I can do to keep them out," he said, desperately thinking about all the doors and windows and wondering which of them were vulnerable and why. "If we get stuck in here, we're going be really trapped. No food, no nothing."

Barry cracked the door open an inch and listened. He couldn't hear anything from downstairs. No matter how smart or weird the pigs were acting, he didn't think they could manage to be stealthy.

"I don't think any have gotten inside yet," he whispered. He slipped out the door before Jenny could respond. He tiptoed into the hall and got the big flashlight, which was perched precariously on the railing.

He closed the door to the balcony quietly and went down the hallway. He was aware of the pain in his foot, but it was distant, less important now. He had so much adrenalin pumping through him, he suspected that it was masking the pain. He'd probably pay for it later, but right then, he was just glad to have his mobility back.

Barry went down the stairs, stopping at every step and listening.

He reached the bottom just as another loud crash echoed through the house and seemed to shake it. He was three steps back up the stairs before he realized it and stopped himself. He gasped for breath then turned it into deep breathing, trying to calm himself. He turned around and went back down the stairs. Despite its loudness, it was clear to him now that the noise was coming from outside.

As he reached the kitchen, something told him not to turn the light on. He could hear the sound of movement outside the sliding glass doors to the patio. He went closer.

Then he turned on his flashlight and turned the beam onto the patio.

It was hard to make sense of it at first. The javelinas were moving around so fast, he couldn't count them. The outside table was upside down, like a turtle, and all the lawn chairs were knocked on their sides. The "Hunter Hacienda" sign was hanging from one hook, and since it was eight feet up, Barry couldn't figure out how it had been knocked askew until he saw one of the bigger pigs spear a chair cushion with its tusk and send it flying into the air.

Then all movement stopped as if the pigs were playing Freeze. They turned their snouts in his direction. Barry started counting them and had reached twenty-five, which wasn't even half of them, when they started moving again. They lined up on either side of the patio, leaving a path down the middle.

Razorback sauntered down their ranks, seemingly in no hurry. He reached the glass door and stared up at Barry, and he realized that the pig could somehow see him behind the flashlight's beam. As he shined the light directly into Razorback's eyes, Barry realized he was thinking of the pig as a "he" instead of an "it" because there was no denying the intelligence in the animal's eyes. The other pigs might all be mindless brutes, but this was a thinking creature. And all his thoughts, it seemed, were turned to chaos and malevolence.

The pig turned away abruptly when the light hit his eyes and trotted to the back of the patio. The other pigs tracked his retreat. Even through the glass, Barry could hear Razorback's urgent grunting. One of the pigs stepped forward, then slowly turned toward the glass door.

Barry was backing away even before the pig started running.

He nearly tripped on the rug his wife kept in front of the sink as the javelina's head smashed into the door. There was a loud crash, and the light of the flashlight shimmered off a crack that was forming like a lightning bolt in the night sky.

Barry turned and ran, but as he passed the pantry, he stopped and shone the light on the rows of food. What would be most useful? What would last the longest? He grabbed a big jar of peanut butter.

Then there was another crash behind him, and all thought of planning went out of his head, and he simply grabbed everything he could carry. He turned and ran up the stairs, dropping cans and boxes of food as he went. He reached the bedroom door and slammed it behind him.

He stood with his back to the door, his breath rasping, his heart pounding so hard he thought it would burst. He listened, waiting for the sound of pursuit. But it was completely silent. Even the noise from outside was gone.

Jenny didn't say a word when he came crashing into the room, nor did she say anything when he crawled into bed next to her. She just reached out with trembling hands and took him in her arms.

Against all odds, Barry went to sleep.

Chapter Thirteen

Razorback's first conscious thought had been *I hate humans.* The desire for revenge radiated from his mother every second of every day, suffusing him with the same revulsion until it overflowed his body and infected everything around him.

His second conscious thought had been the realization that he was different from his siblings. They were more intelligent than the average wild pig, but they didn't seem to have the self-awareness of Razorback and his mother. She ignored the others and focused all her attention on him. His brothers and sisters went off on their own when they were grown, but Razorback stayed with his mother and soaked up her loathing of humans, even though he had never actually met one.

They stayed hidden in a small valley, hundreds of miles from where his mother had escaped from a company farm. Again and again, she described her ordeal to him, and talked about her captors so often that he could visualize them in detail. When he finally did see a human, it was disappointing. It was such a pathetically defenseless creature. He easily killed the man, who didn't even seemed frightened until the last moment, when Razorback rushed forward in a surge of blinding fury and slashed into his thighs, sending blood squirting out in all directions, some of it splashing onto Razorback. He licked the blood and got his first taste of humans. When he returned to the burrow, his mother licked the rest of the blood away, and he wallowed in her approval.

And once again, she told him her story.

She'd first become aware inside a cage, alone. She had no memory of anything before that, no images of her mother or her siblings. There wasn't enough room in the enclosure for her to move around. She remembered insects biting her and blood trickling down her sides, and there'd been nothing she could do, no way to relive the itching and the pain.

On both sides of her were other cages, and there were others beyond them, extending into infinity, and though these cages were filled with creatures that looked like her, smelled like her, and sounded like her, they were mere animals. They had neither her self-awareness nor her intelligence. That may have been a blessing, for they were mad, driven out of their minds by their confinement. She watched one of them get taken away, and then returned, squealing its pleas as it was put back into its cage. It had slumped over and not moved for days, until finally a human had come along and removed the lifeless body.

To one side of her was a pig that was so out of its mind that it squealed hour after hour, day after day, until she hated it and wanted it to die. She watched as the top of her neighbor's cage was lifted and a human arm descended, wearing gloves, and a long object in its hands was inserted into the captive pig. She watched as the pig grew bigger and bigger until it, too, was taken away. It was returned, no longer fat, and after that it was quiet and motionless, as if its mind and spirit were completely gone.

Despite her self-awareness, she did not become insane like the others—or perhaps it was because she could think and plan that she did not lose her mind. Her hatred so consumed her that she could think of nothing else, and her days were filled with visions of humans suffering the same fate as her.

She had become slowly aware that she too was growing larger, though at a slower pace than those around her. The humans sometimes stood in front of her cage and made noises, and she realized they were talking about her, were confused by her. She paid attention to the sounds the humans emitted and, over time, she saw a pattern and began to understand some of what they were saying.

The humans discussed taking her away and turning her into something called "bacon," but in the end, they decided her brood was still alive, though they were taking too long to be born. She was eventually taken to a room that was but a larger cage and fed something—the humans called it "medicine"—and not long afterward, she felt a great pain in her lower body, and out came small versions of herself, squealing and squirming. She looked into their eyes and saw that they were like all the other pigs, not aware of themselves, but simply reacting. All but one. This one stood up on all four legs almost immediately and looked back at her as if to say, *I know you. You are like me.*

But a human came along and lifted out the self-aware one and slit its throat right in front of her.

"I'm not wasting food on a runt," the human said, though she didn't understand all the words.

For the first time in her life, she squealed like the others, was mindless like the others, and she tried to bite the humans as they put her back into her cage. A few days later, the top of the cage lifted just enough for a hand to descend and poke a syringe into her.

Soon after that, she began to feel life growing within her once more. On that day, she began to plan her escape.

The humans would come for her again, she knew. The next time they opened the cage, she would be ready for them. In her anger, she slammed her head against the bars of her cage, again and again, and became aware of her tusks ringing against the metal. She examined her neighbors and saw that none of them had tusks the size and sharpness of hers. In this, too, she was a different creature.

And so she waited, and focused all her hate into her tusks, and practiced wielding them, imagining the soft flesh of the humans in front of her, imagining slicing into them, the blood spraying like the blood of the young one they had killed, the one who had never had a chance to grow. Who had been aware, in those final seconds, of what was happening to him.

She felt the life growing within her. The pigs on either side gave birth to their litters, and then to more litters, but this time, the humans were patient with her, for it seemed that her brood had been bigger and stronger than most of their kind and that she was to be given special treatment.

The day came when the humans lifted the top of her cage. There were three of them, too many for her to fight, so she bided her time. She was taken to a small room and given the same medicine as before, and then left alone.

Finally, a single human came to check on her, and despite the pain in her body, she rose up and slashed out, and it was as she had always imagined. The flesh of the human's neck gave way easily, and blood fountained out of the man so fast that he barely had time to cry out, and then she was running out the door and down a hallway while humans shouted and gave chase. She easily left them behind.

Outside the doors, the vastness of the world had nearly overwhelmed her, but the pain and anger and hate had focused her on the simple act of running, running as far from the humans as she could get. There were shrubs and trees not far from the giant building, and she plunged into them, not knowing what they were, only knowing that she had to escape, to get away from her tormentors, to give her children a chance to live, to be free of the cages, to survive.

She didn't go far before she collapsed in a gully and gave birth. The runt of the litter had been Razorback, and she had given him special attention, pushing away his siblings so he could feed first. Over time, he had grown bigger than the others, and had become aware that he was different in other ways as well. And he had learned hatred of humans from his mother.

He was fully grown on the day his mother didn't return from foraging. He found her body lying in a dry gulch. She had been shot in the head.

Her suffering was over, but she lived on in Razorback. He'd ranged far and wide over their small valley, observing the humans, learning their weaknesses.

When it had come time to breed his own children, he'd selected the biggest wild pig he could find, and to his amazement and delight, all his brood had been like him. As their birthright, he passed down to them the hatred of humans that his mother had taught him, and he began to plan his revenge.

One of the humans had called him Razorback, and he'd adopted the name, finding it suitable. He was Razorback, and he was going to teach the humans what it was like to be at the mercy of another species.

He would teach them fear.

Chapter Fourteen

Mark was the only employee left in the entire hardware store. Christy and Jerad had been there earlier, but both had mysteriously disappeared. Karina hadn't returned from lunch.

Flakes, the whole lot of them. Where Mark came from, you didn't abandon your post no matter what.

But as night began to fall, he started getting nervous. They were supposed to stay open until nine, but they were also supposed to be staffed by no fewer than three employees. Hell, if the boss couldn't even make in, why should he stay?

The irony was he'd probably made more money than the store had ever earned in one day. People had stripped the shelves.

But it was what they were buying that was most alarming: camping gear, guns, knives, ammo, survival gear, propane, nails, and hammers. Like the end of the world was coming. Like it was a zombie apocalypse.

He kept hearing the term javelinas and had to look it up on his cellphone. Some kind of pig, he'd discovered, then his phone service had blinked off.

When the electricity went out in the store right before dark, that was the final straw. Besides, Mark was pretty sure he wasn't supposed to stay open when the lights were out anyway.

He hurriedly locked the front door, counted the till, and dropped the money in the safe. He was headed out the door when he remembered Mr. Pederson's words. "Buy one of your fine wares," he'd said, "and take it home along with a box of ammunition."

Rumor was, the old man was a millionaire and only pretended to be a hick.

Mark turned around. There was only a single rifle left in the entire store, a .30-06, which was fine with him. It was what he was accustomed to using when deer hunting. He took it and a box of shells. He wrote an IOU and slipped it in with his time sheet. He wasn't sure what store policy was about draws because he hated taking them. He might lose his job, but old man Pederson had been pretty compelling.

And *something* was going on.

Mark locked the door behind him and turned around to find the street completely empty: not a soul in sight, not even a moving car. The three guys who were always drinking on the corner and who pestered him for loose change every night, even though he hadn't once given them any, were gone.

What the hell is going on?

He wanted to call Peggy so bad he couldn't stand it. It occurred to him that he'd gotten in the habit of calling her every hour on the hour. He'd heard of Internet withdrawal, but never thought he'd suffer from it. *This isn't Internet withdrawal,* he told himself, *this is Peggy withdrawal.*

He'd followed her down to this hot, dusty, godforsaken place because he was madly in love with her. He'd thought she was so smart, so sophisticated, that wherever she had come from had to be smart and sophisticated too—at least more so than Moscow, Idaho.

He couldn't have been more wrong. There wasn't anyone here but old people.

He slung the rifle strap over his shoulder, feeling silly. Even in Moscow, people didn't usually walk around with guns strapped to their backs. He carried the box of ammunition in his other hand.

It was a five-minute walk to their apartment. The town was tiny, but he'd managed to find a job about as far away from home as he could possibly get. That was okay. It gave him five minutes in the morning to savor the glow of having been in Peggy's presence all night, and it gave him five minutes every night to anticipate being in her presence again. Actually, all he had to do was think of her, and it was as if she was with him. It was as if she had pried open a part of his brain and crawled inside.

Mark smiled at the image. Maybe he should take up drawing again while he was down here. He'd wanted to be a comic book artist for a while, and he actually had some talent. Peggy was always bugging him to start drawing again.

He was so lost in these thoughts that he didn't notice the pig at first. It was standing still in the middle of the sidewalk as if waiting for him. He was a dozen yards away before he saw it.

Weird, Mark thought. *That's something you don't see every day.* But, hey, there were herds of deer wandering around Moscow, so this was probably the same kind of thing. He took another step forward, expecting the animal to run away.

Instead, it lowered its head and took a step toward him.

"Bug off, you mangy critter!" he shouted, waving his arms.

The pig backed up a couple of steps and stared at Mark. The last of the day's light fell on its face, and its expression sent a shock through Mark's chest. He'd seen that look before back when he was delivering newspapers: a mean look, the look a dog gave you when it wanted to chew your leg off.

He swung the gun around. He drew back the bolt then carefully got to his knees and fumbled with the box of ammo. He had pulled out a single cartridge and started to load it when the animal charged. Mark managed to slam the bolt home and take aim.

It wouldn't fire. He'd forgotten to release the safety. It was an amateur mistake, the kind that would cost you a chance at a trophy buck.

The kind that might get you killed.

He didn't look for the safety, just swung the stock with all his might at the charging pig and connected, sending the animal tumbling off the sidewalk into the street. As Mark completed the swing, his finger landed on a familiar-feeling switch, and he flipped it. He managed to turn the barrel toward the pig, who had gotten up and was charging him again, and pull the trigger.

Half of its head disappeared. It flopped off the sidewalk and into the street again. Mark walked over and toed it curiously.

So that's a javelina? It's nothing but a hairy pig.

As if in response to this thought, he heard a grunt, a classic pig grunt like from a cartoon. It was quickly joined by a bunch of other grunts. He turned slowly. Half a block away, a dozen of the creatures were staring him down.

Mark reached down and grabbed the box of ammunition.

Then he turned and ran.

Chapter Fifteen

Barbara Weiss was getting tired of waiting. She knew the pigs wanted to attack. In the late afternoon, one of them walked right up to the window and looked her in the eye. It wasn't a dumb animal that stared at her but another intelligent being. A mean one.

She recognized the look. She'd seen it in the eyes of the psychopaths she'd been lucky enough to catch and put away. Worse, she'd seen it in the eyes of the smarter psychopaths she hadn't been able to convict and put away.

There was a breakdown in authority in this county. Barbara recognized the signs. Once, in her old job, when a wildfire had nearly consumed the west side of the neighboring town of Redmond, the sheriff of that county had called in a panic. He was completely ineffectual, and she'd driven the thirty miles in ten minutes and taken over. But meanwhile, the criminals had been free to do their damndest while the other town officials tried to control the panic. Things never should have got that far, but it had happened.

No one was in charge here. There had been that tone in the 9-1-1 operator's voice, the one that said she was scared and didn't know what to do and that there was no one who could tell her.

To hell with it, Barbara thought. *I'm retired.*

Besides, there was no chance that they'd let some strange woman take over. It had been bad enough in Crook County, where she'd had decades of experience to back her up.

She had thirty-six bullets left in the box and fifteen in her clip. There was another clip in the glove box of the car, and she decided to go get it.

She opened the door warily, but there wasn't a pig to be seen. She walked quickly down the walkway. She'd learned from experience to move steadily, with economy of motion, and that she'd get the job done faster and more efficiently that way than if she hurried. She got to the car, opened the passenger door, opened the glove box, and reached in for the clip. She was keeping an eye and ear out for the pigs, so when one came around the corner and stopped dead in its tracks, she watched it carefully.

It raised its snout and squealed.

Barbara put the clip in her pocket and turned to walk back to the house. She sensed a single javelina wouldn't attack her. But fifteen would. They came around the side of the house at a full run. She stopped, and her training took over as she assessed the threat. *Moving target: friend or foe? Well, this is easy. All foes.*

She dropped one then another then a third. Several of the others tripped and tumbled over their dead mates. Barbara killed the lead pig each time, and that seemed to sink into their consciousness because suddenly, none of them were in a hurry to be first.

Then the intelligent javelina, The Mean One, came around the corner, staying well back. It grunted commands, and the other pigs surged forward again.

Barbara had been slowly retreating toward the house the whole time. She was halfway there when the javelinas charged. Again, she stopped and faced off with the pigs. She fired steadily, picking them off one by one, and it was a slaughter.

Then she missed, and in the second it took her to fire again, the nearest animal was five feet closer. The others followed. She missed again, and now, they were ten feet closer. She tried to keep the panic down, to fire steadily, but her nerves overrode her brain, and she missed two more times even at that close range.

Then she was clicking on an empty chamber. She turned and ran for the open door, pulling the extra clip out of her pocket and sliding it home as she ran. She felt a sharp pain in her right leg and staggered.

Fuck it, she thought. *If I'm going to get killed by pigs, it won't be while running from them.*

She stopped, and several of the pigs went barreling past her and had to turn around.

Suddenly, it was as if she could see and hear everything at once. Her hand was steady, and it seemed as if it moved in a blur. *Blam, blam, blam.* The rest of the javelinas went down.

Barbara turned to where she'd last noticed The Mean One, but it was already running away. She wasted the last five bullets in her clip trying to hit it, but it was gone.

She limped into the house and slammed the door. Her legs began shaking so badly, she had to sit down on the small rug in the entryway. She felt dizzy. She looked down at her leg. It didn't hurt, but her entire pants leg was soaked with blood. *I'm going to bleed out*, she thought.

Barbara pulled out her belt, circled her upper thigh with it, and cinched it as tight as she could. Holding onto the belt, keeping up the pressure, she made it to the bathroom. There was a jar of superglue there and some scissors.

She cut away her trousers and groaned when she saw the deep gash in her calf. She squeezed the cut together, practically poured glue over it, and held on.

Minutes passed, and Barbara wasn't sure if she lost consciousness or not, but somehow, she managed to hold the wound closed. When she finally let go, her glue-covered fingers pulled some skin away, but the cut stayed glued shut.

Then she keeled over on the bathroom mat and passed out.

Pain woke her. She'd let go of the tourniquet while she slept, but it didn't matter. She hadn't lost any more blood. She'd survive if the injury didn't get infected, and she had enough antibiotics to keep that from happening. She needed to drink plenty of fluids for a while, but she hadn't lost so much blood that she was incapacitated.

She washed down some pills with a big glass of water. Then she took off what was left of her pants, cleaned herself up as best she could, and wrapped some bandages around the wound.

Exhausted, Barbara limped her way to bed. Before she fell asleep, it occurred to her that in her attempt to get a clip of fifteen bullets, she had expended thirty bullets for a net loss of fifteen.

She laughed. It had been worth it.

It had been the most terrifying, the most exhilarating, the most *fun* experience she'd had in Arizona. And she'd shown the pigs what's what.

She figured they'd think twice before testing her again.

Chapter Sixteen

"Three jars of olives?" Jenny asked.

"Sorry," Barry said. "I just grabbed anything I could."

She laughed then went over and gave him a hug. "I know. I was only teasing. I can't believe how brave you were to go down there."

"Brave...or hungry?" he said, smiling.

In the morning, everything looked less terrifying. From their bedroom window, there wasn't a javelina in sight, and there were no sounds from downstairs.

"I don't think they made it inside," he said. "I'm going to check."

"No!" Jenny cried. "Stay here. Let's stick to our plan, just wait it out. I *love* olives you know."

"I'll be careful," Barry promised. He cracked the door open before she could protest again. He stuck his nose out and sniffed. No pig smell. No grunts. No banging and crashing. He still didn't think the pigs were canny enough to lay a trap, though after last night's events, he wasn't absolutely sure.

He hurried downstairs, being as quiet as he could, the heavy flashlight in his hands despite the brightness of the day.

He stepped into the kitchen, flashlight raised. The room was empty. It occurred to him that he might be able to find another weapon. He opened the drawer next to the oven. There it was, the massive butcher knife he'd given to Jenny one Christmas, which, as far he knew, had never been used. *All the sharper for it*, he thought. He transferred the flashlight to his left hand and grabbed the knife. Only then did he approach the sliding glass doors.

The crack ran nearly the entire perpendicular length of the door. Right outside laid a dead pig, its neck broken by the impact.

Barry almost didn't recognize the patio or the backyard. Everything was broken beyond repair. The umbrella, which had been over the table, was in shreds. Every flower and bush had been pulled out of the ground, and though he could still see hints of green in the lawn, most of it was torn up.

There was pig shit everywhere.

"That's fucking intentional," he said aloud, somehow more offended by that than anything else he'd seen. "You creepy animals."

He put his finger to the crack. The door was double paned, and the crack was on the outside pane. Barry supposed he should have been reassured, but he wasn't. How long before old Razorback convinced a few more of his followers to commit hara-kiri?

He heard a sound behind him and whirled, knife raised.

Jenny was staring at the chaos outside with wide eyes. "What did we ever do to them?" she asked, sounding offended.

"Seems to me we provided them with a daily banquet," he said. "A veritable buffet."

She shook her head, absentmindedly picking up the dropped containers of food. When her hands were full, she pulled out a fresh trash bag from below the sink and dropped the food inside. She went to the pantry and continued to fill the bag then went and got another bag and started filling it too.

Without a word, Barry picked up the first bag of food and took it upstairs to the bedroom. While he was there, he filled the bathtub with water not to bathe in but because so far, the pigs had been one step ahead of them, and he didn't know what the animals were capable of. Barry didn't know how they could cut off the water, but that's what worried him—not knowing.

When he went back downstairs, Jenny was looking thoughtfully through the knives, one by one, hefting them. A little bit of a chill went down his spine, but he didn't say anything. He wished they could do better for weapons. He'd always been anti-gun, and it burned his ass that the gun nuts might have been right—about Armageddon at least.

With that thought in mind, he went to the garage. The garage was full of junk, which was why—unfortunately—the car was parked out of reach outside. But it also gave him the chance of finding something useful. *All this junk was saved for some reason*, he thought. *For the day we needed it. Well, today's the day.*

But it turned out that none of the junk was much use in a pig apocalypse.

A porkocalypse, Barry thought and smiled. *A hamaggedon.*

He found a hammer and decided that it made more sense as a weapon than a flashlight especially considering he wouldn't be risking smashing the bulb and making the flashlight useless.

There was a sheet of corrugated metal against one wall from when he'd thought of building a shed. That was when he was still thinking like a Bendite and believed he'd need to protect his equipment from the snow. He wrestled it into the house, took it upstairs, and leaned it against the bedroom wall. Then he went to the garage again and rummaged around until he found some nails. They were roofing nails, but there was a full container of them, and he thought they'd do the job.

Meanwhile, Jenny had managed to get most of the food upstairs.

"You think we're going to be here for months?" he asked.

"Never hurts to be prepared," she said cheerfully. "Or maybe I just want a choice in my meals."

Barry trotted down the stairs, and at the bottom, it suddenly occurred to him what he'd just done. He hadn't walked down the stairs. *No, worse*, he thought. *I didn't trudge down the stairs.* He had nearly skipped down them, humming a happy tune. He shook his head at the mystery of it all, went back into the garage, and started piling boxes on the floor, making a total mess of things, looking for something useful for the next few nights.

He was sure the authorities would rescue them by the end of the day or at least by tomorrow. But if they had to spend another night there, he wanted to be prepared.

Suddenly, Bend, Oregon, with all its hipsters and snow, wasn't looking so bad. Especially because there was one thing the town lacked: javelinas. There was the occasional cougar, perhaps, but cougars were sensible enough to run when given the chance.

When he finally gave up his Easter egg hunt, Jenny was back in the kitchen, at the stove, cooking some ham and eggs. "Might be our last chance at a hot meal," she said. She too was humming, and it occurred to Barry that the danger had brought them together, given them a purpose, and that both of them were enjoying it.

Still…there ought to be an easier way. When this was all over, he was going to try harder to find activities they both enjoyed and that had more meaning than card games and pickleball.

They sat at the dining room table for once. They didn't even glance at the TV though it passed through Barry's mind that perhaps there was some news there, or on the radio, about their situation. *I'll check right after breakfast*, he thought. *Or lunch. Or brunch or whatever this is.* Whatever it was, it was nice just to be sitting there with Jenny.

They sat eating quietly, trying to ignore the mess outside. There wasn't a javelina to be seen. It was beginning to seem like it had been a bad dream and that it was now over. The sun was bright, the sky was a clear blue, and there was nothing threatening in sight.

After brunch, Barry got up and turned on the TV. There was nothing but snowy reception. He switched off the cable connection and tried to get reception the old-fashioned way: over the air. He could sometimes get the nearest channel though not clearly.

He found it, turned up the volume, and tried to make sense of the words through the static. It was the local weatherman, but he was sitting at the anchor's desk.

"Stay indoors," the man was saying. "I repeat; stay indoors. Help is on the way."

And with that, the TV blinked off. In the background, the refrigerator went silent. It always let out a low hum, which Barry was aware of but which was part of the normal background noise. The sudden absence of the hum was impossible to ignore.

"The bastards cut the electricity," Jenny said.

"I don't see how that's possible. Those are overhead lines."

He went to the corner of the house that overlooked the electrical pole and saw wires hanging down, sparking as they waved in the wind.

How the hell did they do that? he wondered.

Jenny was standing at the patio door. Barry wanted to tell her to get away from it, but he didn't want to scare her. He hurried to her side, planning to move her gently back. Then he saw what she was staring at.

What looked like a hundred of the pigs were chasing a dog. It was sprinting with all its might for their patio door.

Before he could stop her, Jenny opened the door. She gave him a look that said, "Don't argue."

The golden retriever—though it was so filthy it was hard to recognize its breed—shot through the opening. Jenny slammed the door shut and latched it as the first javelina slid into the glass. The outside panel of glass shattered, and the pig squealed as broken shards rained down on it. Thankfully, the inner panel stayed in place. A large piece of glass plunged into the pig's neck, and it fell on its side and twitched once, twice, and was still.

Supposed to be safety glass, Barry thought. *Isn't supposed to do that.*

The pigs were milling about outside, pushing each other aside, sometimes leaping over their fellows in a twirling, jumbled mass. Then they suddenly went quiet and lined up in neat rows again almost as if they were deliberately forming ranks, as impossible as that seemed.

Razorback walked down the middle of his lined-up fellows and looked at the two humans. He stared up at them with calm, yellow eyes. Then he casually turned and walked away. To Barry, he seemed to be saying, *I can get you anytime. You're just meat in a can.*

"What was that?" Jenny cried, and Barry realized that she hadn't met old Razorback before.

"That, my dear, is the cause of all our troubles." A glimmer of an idea rose in the back of his mind. *Take out the leader,* he thought. But the idea was so outrageous, so desperate, that he dismissed it.

Like the guy on TV said, help is on the way, he reassured himself.

Except…why had it been the weatherman? And why had the studio been so empty, and why had the camera been at such an odd angle? And why had he sounded as if the microphone was yards away?

The dog had flopped onto its side the moment it was inside and was breathing hard. It looked up at them with trusting but panicked eyes.

"That's the Underwoods' dog," Jenny said. "What do you think happened?"

Barry looked at the blood all over the dog's normally silky fur and what looked like bits of meat and gristle stuck to it. He didn't tell Jenny where he thought the Underwoods—or at least part of them—were.

"Do we have any candles?" he asked.

Chapter Seventeen

Barry tried the faucet with some trepidation, but the water was still flowing. They washed off the whining dog as best they could. He felt for the tag around its neck and checked it.

"Welcome to our humble abode, Aragorn," he said to the dog, who with the name became a "he." The dog wagged his tail at the sound of his name.

They fed him a can of stew; it was the best they could do, being a non-pet household. Aragorn went to the corner of the living room—about as far from the four walls of the house as he could get—curled up, and went to sleep.

"Where is the help?" Jenny asked, which was the same thing Barry was thinking. "Police, firefighters? Shit, where's the army?"

"Watch your mouth, woman," he growled then smiled.

She didn't return the smile. "No, really. What the *hell?* A few machine guns and they could take care of this problem."

"Unless we've been cut off," he said. "Cell phone towers, cables, everything."

"That's crazy."

"Well…" He raised his hands in mock surrender. "But think about our little neck of the woods. We're completely isolated. No phone, no Internet. They've got us trapped. Maybe this is more widespread than we've been thinking."

"Thinking? I wasn't *thinking* anything. I just thought our neighborhood javelinas had gotten out of control. Until…until I saw that *beast.*" Jenny shuddered.

"Yeah, old Razorback is a sight to behold," Barry agreed. "He's a mutant or something. But…he still has hoofs, not opposable thumbs. I don't think he's anything but a very, very, *very* smart pig."

"Smarter than us, apparently," she said.

Barry started laughing, and Jenny looked sheepish at first then joined him. It was gallows humor, maybe, but it still felt good to laugh.

"What do we do now?" she asked.

"Stay put, like the man said. Though…"

"Though what?"

"Well, I heard somewhere that in times of disaster, the best thing to do is move around. Get out of the trouble area."

"You think it's that bad?"

"Nah," Barry said, sounding more cheerful than he felt. "How could it be? They're just pigs."

Barry and Jenny didn't really need the candles. They went to bed almost immediately after dark. They'd only been under the covers for a few moments before they heard whining and scratching at the door. They let Aragorn in, and he jumped up onto the foot of the bed and lay down between their feet.

Neither of them objected. It felt comforting to have the animal there. *Besides*, Barry thought, *he's the best early warning system we could have.*

Strangely, nothing happened during the night. There wasn't even a grunt or a snort; the javelinas left them alone. But when they woke up in the morning, the sky was full of smoke. It was coming from every direction as if every other house in the subdivision was on fire.

When they'd first moved there, Barry had loved the isolation. Now, he was regretting it.

They made a cold breakfast, deciding to eat as much of the perishables as quickly as they could. Aragorn whined and wound around their feet, nearly tripping them more than once, before Jenny suddenly cried out with a slap to the head, "He needs to go potty!"

They looked around helplessly. Finally, Barry took the dog to the garage. Aragorn looked at him doubtfully but eventually found a spot in the corner and did his business. After that, he was friskier and friendlier than ever as if he'd forgotten there was ever any danger.

"You know what?" Jenny said after giving the dog a hug. "After this, I'd like to get a dog. I know you're worried about your garden…"

Barry pointed out the back window at the bare dirt and tangles of roots. "You mean *that* garden? I agree, Jenny, let's get a dog. And a cat too, dammit."

"Maybe we can keep…" She suddenly stopped as if realizing by saying it out loud, she was admitting the Underwoods were dead.

"Yeah, maybe," he said softly.

A couple of times during the morning, Aragorn growled, and they tensed, got up, and looked out the window fearfully. But each time, it was a single javelina or only a small pack.

It all seemed very strange. They were now in the third day of not hearing from the outside world. By this time, the whole world should have been alerted that something bizarre was happening in their little corner of Arizona.

Maybe they have been, Barry thought with sudden chill. *Maybe everyone else has already been saved. Maybe the authorities have just forgotten about us.*

Hamilton wouldn't let that happen.

With that thought, Barry froze.

No…he *wouldn't* let that happen. So that meant that something had happened to Hamilton, and if it could happen to the Animal Control officer, it could happen to anyone. It could happen to them.

At that moment, Barry knew that it would be a mistake to stay another moment.

"I need a broom handle," Barry said.

Jenny didn't question his request. She went to the pantry and returned with a broom. His last birthday present to her had been hiring a local maid service. Too late, he'd discovered that that only made Jenny madly clean the house the day before the cleaners showed up. No amount of pleading would keep her from doing it. "Just a little touchup," she'd say. "I don't want to be embarrassed."

Barry broke off the brush end of the broom, hobbled to the kitchen, and tried several knives on the wood before finding one sharp enough to do the job. He whittled the end to a sharp point in short order, trepidation giving his arms and fingers the strength to carve long slivers out of the wood.

Jenny and Aragorn watched him for a while.

"What are you doing?" she asked finally.

"Making a spear," he said.

"I can see that," she said when he didn't look up. "*Why* are you making a spear?"

"Just extra protection," he said.

"Dear husband of mine," she said, and he finally looked at her. "When you won't look me in the eye, I know you're lying. That's always been your tell. I'm telling you this so that you'll realize how serious I am, giving up the little advantage I've had over you all these years: knowing when you're lying. I will ask again; *why* are you making a spear?"

"I need to go get help," Barry said. "Razorback is toying with us. He can get in any time. All he has to do is send one of his minions headfirst into the glass, and he's in. How long will our bedroom door hold up? How are we going to defend ourselves with knives and a hammer?"

"I agree," Jenny said, completely surprising him. "But…"

He looked up from his whittling again.

"Why does it have to be you? I can drive a car as fast as you can…faster, frankly."

"Nope," he said. "That's not the way it's going to be."

"Why not? Why should you do the dangerous thing? Because you're a man?"

"No!" he said loudly, and he could see she was taken aback. He'd rarely yelled at her during their marriage. Moreover, he usually acceded to her demands. "It isn't about being a man or a woman. It's about being you and me."

She didn't say anything, simply waited for him to continue.

"Because without me…you'll still be all right." She started to object, and he held up his hand. "Oh, you'd be sad, I know that. You might be devastated, but you know what? You'd get on with life. You're tough, sensible. It would hurt, but there would still be life in you."

"What about you? You've got as much…"

"No," he said, firmly. "Without you, I'm lost. I've always known it. I've dreaded it. Every day of my life with you, I've been thankful that you plucked me out of my hermitage…" Again, she opened her mouth to object, and he put his fingers on her lips to shush her. "It's true. You may not believe it, but I've always known. I don't want to be alone, Jenny. And that's what would happen."

"You don't know that," she said softly.

"Yeah. I do."

She didn't say anything more because they both knew that, as fucked up as it may have seemed, he was right.

Chapter Eighteen

The pigs are herding me, Mark realized. Away from his apartment, away from Peggy. He stopped and loaded the rifle then poured the rest of the bullets into his pocket, where he could get at them more easily.

Two can play at that game, he thought.

Every time pigs got in his way, he lifted the rifle and fired. He hit his target every time. He'd always been a good shot. He spent hours at the shooting range in an old cinderblock building at the edge of town, wearing earmuffs, shooting at targets on wires, then pulling them back and checking his score.

He was lucky; this rifle was miraculously zeroed in. Either that or it was miraculously compensating for his being off target.

Mark smiled grimly. He still couldn't believe these pig creatures could hurt him. But he'd seen the tusks on the first one he killed, so he was wary.

The javelinas were herding Mark toward the mouth of an alley. He stood his ground, sensing that if they managed to corner him in there, he was done for. He shot a charging javelina and reloaded in seconds. He was getting pretty good at it.

His ammo was half gone. What was left rattled in his pocket, but all he wanted to do was make it home.

He'd started to walk away from the alley when he saw the body just a few feet in. That was shocking enough, but when he saw the red coat, he nearly buckled at the knees.

Joe Sanders was the manager of the hardware store. A loud, garish kind of guy but nice as could be. He wore a red sports coat to work. Called it his uniform. His signature look.

Now, his face was as red as his coat. His trousers were red

too. His viscera spread out all over the alley was red and yellow and…

Mark leaned over and threw up.

A javelina took the opportunity to charge. He straightened up and blew the creature backward. Then he kept marching toward the pack, firing and reloading, firing and reloading, killing one of the pigs with every step.

When there were only two left, they bolted.

Mark turned around and trotted straight for his apartment, gun at the ready. Twice more, he saw one of the javelinas; twice more, he fired and hit.

His pocket was no longer jingling with bullets when he reached the grocery store. Peggy worked there and usually got off a couple of hours before he did. They'd gotten a sweet deal on the apartment above the store, so much so that even though neither of them was earning much more than minimum wage, they were managing to save some money.

The money was for sending him to art school, or so Peggy thought.

But it was really for buying a ring and getting married. That's what Mark thought.

The door on the side of the grocery was unlocked, and he entered warily then realized there was no way the damn pigs could turn the knob. He stopped and counted the remaining bullets. Fourteen out of fifty. How was that possible? It seemed to him that he'd rarely missed his target. How many of those monsters were there? Why did they keep throwing themselves at him?

What the hell was going on?

He looked down at his trousers. They were his work pants, the only pants he owned that weren't jeans. The bottoms of them were covered with mud, blood, and viscera. How was he going to explain that to Peggy?

He tromped up the stairs and tried to open the door. It was locked. He was stunned. It was never locked.

"Peggy?" he said, in a low, curious voice.

The door flew open, and Peggy grabbed him by the hand and pulled him inside. Not until she'd slammed the door shut and turned the lock did she throw herself into his arms.

"Thank God you're home," she gasped.

And Mark knew he didn't have to explain the blood and the mud and the gore.

Chapter Nineteen

"We have a spare set of keys, don't we?" Barry asked.

Jenny went to the junk drawer and rummaged around. She pulled out a key and, with a wrinkled nose, handed it to him. "I *think* that is the right one."

"Think?"

"Pretty sure..."

It would have to do. If he had time, he intended to grab her purse along the way, so it might be a moot issue.

Barry wasn't actually as scared as he probably should have been. They had seen very few javelinas about. It seemed unlikely they could magically appear out of nowhere before he was able to get away—which made him wonder: Where had they gone?

Old Razorback was smarter than that. What did he know that Barry didn't?

Only one way to find out. Barry's spear was as sharp as he could make it. His large butcher knife was in his belt, at his side, and he was hoping he wouldn't poke himself with it.

"One last thing," Barry said. He took Jenny by the hand and led her upstairs. He handed her the hammer and the container of roofing nails. "As soon as I'm gone, I want you to nail this sheet of metal to the doorframe. Use a nail every couple inches; don't be stingy. I'm thinking even old Razorback might have a hard time getting in."

"What about Aragorn?" she asked.

"Leave him outside the door. He'll let you know when they're coming. Might be able to take out a few of them. Right, Aragorn? Eh, Strider?" Barry knelt, and the dog practically leaped into his arms. "Take care of her," he whispered.

He looked up at his wife, who had tears in her eyes. He knew she wouldn't leave Aragorn outside, but he'd had to try.

They hugged and kissed, and he wanted nothing more, at that moment, than to take her back to bed and make love to her one more time. But he broke away and started down the stairs. She followed him.

"I mean it," he said without turning around. "Barricade yourself in before dark."

"I promise."

Aragorn followed them as far as the entryway to the front door then stopped and looked agitated. He barked once, and Barry shushed him and, being an apparently well-trained dog, he became quiet.

There wasn't a lot of planning in what Barry was doing. Open the door, run for the car, snag his wife's purse along the way, drive the car to town, and get help. That was it. So easy...and so hard. He decided against a last goodbye because he was certain if he turned around and hugged his wife, he wouldn't leave.

He opened the door quietly and walked quickly down the walkway. He grabbed Jenny's purse and kept going, trying to ignore the parts of Peter still strewn about. For some reason, the swine had left his head untouched, and it was swelling in the heat. It looked ready to burst.

Barry made it to the car without any trouble, looked in Jenny's purse, found the keys, and started the car. He looked down at the gas gauge. The tank was full. He couldn't believe how easy it was. Why had they been cowering in the house all this time when this was all they had to do?

He started driving, but he hadn't gone more than few feet before he realized something was wrong. The car moved sluggishly and swerved sideways then jerked to the other side. He dared to roll down the window. He looked down and saw two things. The first was that the tires were completely shredded. The second was a wave of javelinas coming down the street toward him.

Barry got out, but instead of running back to the house, he sprinted toward Peter's Toyota SUV, which was parked at the curb. He couldn't see the tires yet, and he was pretty sure what he'd find when he could, but he had to find out.

The SUV was low to the ground, the tires so cut up that the vehicle was almost resting on the rims. Barry didn't stop because the wave of javelinas was coming fast. He grabbed the door, praying it wasn't locked, and slipped inside. He slammed the door as the first of the pigs crashed into it and then another. He could see the dents from the inside.

The pigs milled about the car, and then one got on its hind legs and looked in the driver's side window, and what Barry saw then chilled him more than anything else he'd seen.

This javelina's eyes were shining with intelligence, just like Razorback's. It seemed almost amused. *So it isn't only a single pig*, Barry thought. Where there were two, there were probably multitudes. And if they could communicate, who knew what they could accomplish? Technology was great, but native cunning could go a long way, especially against prey that was fat and complacent, that hadn't had to fend for themselves in generations.

Humans had always prided themselves on being different than other animals, but maybe it was only a difference of degrees, and the gap between the degrees had just shrunk.

Meanwhile, Barry thought, *this human of perhaps a little above average intelligence is trapped.*

He knew that vehicles could be driven on their rims. It wasn't good for them and would probably wreck them for future use, but there *was* no future for him if he didn't get out of there. He figured the SUV could go for a ways. But without the keys, he couldn't even get it to do that.

He searched the glove box and the visors. Nothing. He sat back and huffed in frustration. *Out of the frying pan and into the fire.*

The only good thing was that the pigs couldn't get at him as long as he was in the SUV—at least, he didn't think they could. They'd have a hard time getting a good angle on the glass to break it, so brute force wouldn't work.

As he was thinking that, feeling a tiny bit safe, he saw the intelligent pig go to the side of the road and pick up a rock with its teeth. It swung its head, and the rock came flying toward Barry and slammed against the door, mere inches below the window.

Barry could have sworn the pig was measuring the distance. If it had been a human, the creature would have raised his fingers and blurred his eyes and tried to calculate it. The pig tossed a second rock that smashed against the window, which by some miracle didn't crack. Barry knew that when it did, the whole window would give way. They were designed that way, to break into tiny pieces.

He ran his hand along the bottom of the seat. He didn't know what compelled him to do that, but the instinct was right. He felt the keys, tucked into the folds of the seat.

He pulled them out and tried the bigger of the two, and the SUV started. When he began to drive away, the vehicle groaned as if it was alive, the motor whined, and he could see sparks shooting from the rims.

He had to turn around, and when he turned the steering wheel, the SUV kept sliding forward on the asphalt for a few yards, sending up even more sparks. When it came to a full stop, he tried again, steering a little less abruptly, and the rims took hold, and the vehicle slowly turned.

The javelinas had simply watched at first, but as he headed downhill, they began to follow him. They didn't even have to run at the pace he was going, just trot behind him. The smart pig loped along beside Barry, and when he caught its eye, it seemed to leer at him.

Must be my imagination, Barry thought. *Pigs don't wink, do they?*

The SUV picked up speed as Barry steered it downhill, but the minute he hit an upslope, it began to slow, losing traction. He barely made it over that hill, so when he saw the next one looming, he tried to accelerate despite the alarming amount of sparks it sent off.

The engine was laboring and edging into the red. Unlike his wife's car, this SUV had had only a quarter of a tank of gas to start with, and the extra friction seemed to be drawing down on that quickly.

The pigs were still keeping pace, and he was a long way from town.

Chapter Twenty

The SUV's engine started smoking first, and then Barry felt the heat and smelled the flames from beneath the vehicle. The sparks had set fire to the oil and grease on the undercarriage. The wheel rims were also getting off kilter, and the SUV was wobbling. The vehicle wasn't going much faster than a walk now, and the pigs were sprinting ahead in their excitement and then circling back.

It wouldn't be long now. All Barry had accomplished with his gambit was to get farther away from shelter.

He stopped the SUV. He had to do something. It was either burn to death or be eaten by pigs, and he wasn't sure which was worse.

I guess panic will decide, he thought, *in those last moments of life.*

No, fuck that. He wasn't through. He looked out the back window. The trailer carrying the motorcycle had four-foot-high walls and was two feet off the ground. It was a good six feet tall altogether. He doubted a pig could jump that high. The sides had wide slats, but they were metal, and it looked to him like the animals probably wouldn't be able to do much more than push their snouts through the gaps.

If he could climb back there, he'd be in a cage, but at least he'd be away from the fire. He opened the glove box, praying there was a glass punch. There it was, a little screwdriver-shaped tool. He turned around and pushed the punch against the back window. It shattered.

The javelinas went crazy when he poked his head out. The gap between the front of the trailer and the SUV was wide enough that the pigs could get a foot and a half in on either side, but Barry realized there was a two-foot-wide area in the middle where they couldn't get to him.

Never had he regretted his two-hundred-pound body more than now. But…well, the weight was actually pretty well distributed. So he'd always told himself; now, it was being put to the test. *No doubt I've lost a good ten or fifteen pounds over the last few days,* he thought. Which only reminded him how hungry and thirsty he was.

The heat was getting uncomfortable. There was nothing for it but to try. He squirmed his way out, barely able to fit through the window. He was wiggling from side to side, and he felt a nip on one arm then the other. One of the pigs got a good grip on his shirt and started pulling him out of the safe zone. He held on tight to the frame of the trailer, and the shirt ripped before his grip broke.

Barry made it the rest of the way and tumbled headfirst into the trailer.

The bike was in the exact middle, and the safest place for him quickly proved to be sitting on its seat.

The fire in the SUV was really taking off now, sending sputtering oil into the air, some of which landed on him and burned through his shirt and trousers. He'd bought himself a few minutes at best.

He looked down at his hands. He still had the keys gripped tightly in one fist, so tightly that, when he opened that hand, he saw that they'd left a white imprint on his palm. There were two keys, he realized, one of them smaller than the other.

Jesus, when was the last time he'd ridden a motorcycle?

Here's where he got really lucky. Barry realized he'd been lucky all along, but this was the thing that saved him. The rack holding the motorcycle was positioned so that the wheels were off the ground. When he found the ignition switch, the wheels turned freely. He experimented with the clutch and the handle grips, and it all came back to him. He was pretty sure he could do it.

He unfastened the motorcycle from the rack. He had to turn the bike around, and he levered it on its rear tire and managed to maneuver it so it was facing the back of the trailer. Now, all that separated him from the road was a single latch on the trailer's gate.

He revved the engine and was reaching for the latch when he saw the leader of the javelinas come trotting over from off to one side, grunting what sounded like orders. The pigs massed behind the gate, and Barry realized he'd land right in the middle of them.

It was only going to get worse, he realized. He couldn't afford to hesitate. He unhooked the latch and shot out of the trailer on the motorcycle, flying over most of the assembled animals, landing on the backs of a couple more, and then he was on the asphalt and roaring away.

He heard whooping and hollering then realized it was him.

It was the most exciting moment of his life.

Chapter Twenty-One

When Pederson came to, the only thing that hurt was his little finger. The air bag had exploded out the front window and had apparently also broken his smallest digit.

How did that happen? he wondered, dazed.

Somehow, he had ended up on the passenger side of the truck. He must have unlatched his seat belt earlier in an unconscious effort to get away. He reached for the door handle and winced at the pain. He used his left hand instead and tumbled out onto the road. He was disoriented for a moment then got to his hands and knees. A shooting pain in his finger made him cry out.

He staggered to his feet, holding the hand immobile and close to his body. He reached into the cab. The glove box opened at a slant, getting stuck halfway down on the right side, but it opened enough for Pederson to reach in with his left hand and pull out the first aid kit. He immobilized his finger, and it immediately stopped hurting as much. He realized that half the pain had been coming from the anticipation of treating it, and now that it was safely wrapped, his brain was relenting.

The second thing he looked for was his gun. He'd had it on the seat next to him. But search as he might, he couldn't find it anywhere.

The box containing the bow and arrow was lying in the middle of the road as if beckoning him. He walked over and picked it up and, while he was at it, kicked some other scattered items and debris out of the road and over the side of the cliff, like a good citizen.

Just in time, for as he was finishing up, he heard sirens approaching. Two fire trucks came swerving around the corner followed by a sheriff's car. The first fire truck slowed down, but he waved it on, and both the trucks kept going.

The deputy stopped. "You okay, Mr. Pederson?"

Pederson recognized Steve Altman, one of the few residents of the valley who knew about Pederson's past. He'd been a security guard in Silicon Valley. He'd gotten in trouble once for falling asleep on the job, and Pederson had gone to bat for him, saving his job. So when he'd become a deputy and gotten a job locally, it hadn't been hard to convince him to stay quiet.

"I'm good, Steve," Pederson told him. "There is nothing you can do here. I'll call the tow truck."

"You sure?"

Pederson nodded. "What's going on?"

"The Silversteins' house is on fire," Altman said. "It sounds bad."

"You better get going then."

The deputy nodded, waved, and accelerated away.

It wasn't until he was long gone that Pederson realized the other casualty of the wreck was his cellphone, which was broken right down the middle.

He calculated the distances. He figured it was six miles to his house by road and three miles over land.

He glanced back at the truck. It was totaled, but most of the supplies inside had survived. If someone was desperate enough to steal them, they were welcome to have them. The supplies had been overstock, really; just stuff he'd bought to fill his truck because he had the room and the money.

Pederson stepped to the side of the road. There was a steep cliff, about fifty feet high, then a few rolling hills, and then the bottom of the valley. If he headed up the dry creek from there, it would be smooth sailing to his place.

There was the outline of a deer trail to his left that he thought he could probably negotiate, and he set off that way. Then, at the last second, he turned around and grabbed the box with the bow and arrows.

It wasn't an easy descent. He was starting to feel his age. His legs were getting wobbly. His right hand was pretty useless in stabilizing him, and the box was bulky. Finally, he let the box slide the final few yards and slid down the rest of the way on his butt. His tailbone hit a rock on the way down, and he gasped for breath for a few minutes while excruciating pain shot through his back. He almost passed out.

The pain eventually passed, leaving a dull ache.

Pederson lay on his side and opened the box, taking out the pieces one by one and examining them. He unfolded the instructions. His engineer's brain quickly made sense of them, and he was able to assemble the bow without much trouble.

He stood up.

Stringing it was a bit harder not because he didn't know what to do but because of his diminishing energy and strength and his immobile finger.

There were twelve arrows in the quiver, which he thought was pretty generous. Everything had a high-tech gleam to it, a pleasing design, and Pederson's Silicon Valley persona appreciated the beautiful functionality of it. This wasn't one of those high-priced bullshit objects that had been made just for looks and brand-name bragging rights; this weapon was the real deal. He could feel it.

He nocked an arrow and tried pulling it back. *Oomph.* The pull was a little much. He perused the instructions again, adjusted the bow, and was able to draw the arrow, but it was awkward.

He unwrapped the bandage around his right hand, almost crying out from the pain, and rewrapped it so that his first two fingers were free. Now, he could draw the arrow much more easily, and though it was tough to get full extension, he knew that the more powerful the pull, the more force the arrow would have and the greater the distance it would fly.

Pederson took aim at what he gauged to be an eight-inch-circumference fir tree about twenty feet away and loosed the arrow. He jerked the bow as he shot, and the arrow went flying far to the left. He marked its location and tried again. This time, he released the arrow as smoothly as if he was pulling the trigger of a gun.

It was inordinately pleasing that he missed by only a few inches.

He sensed the gun analogy was the right one. Draw the arrow back, take a deep breath, let it out slowly, and release…

He tracked down the two arrows, put one back on the bowstring and the other in the quiver, and started off.

Pederson was only a few hundred yards along when he realized he'd made an enormous—and avoidable—mistake. It was a hot Arizona afternoon, and he was sweating profusely. And getting thirstier with every step.

Like an idiot, he'd left gallons of bottled water in his truck.

He contemplated going back but was pretty sure that he'd have a hard time making it up the cliff, especially with the bow, and he wasn't willing to relinquish it. Better to stay on the flats and make a beeline for his house and barn. *A couple more miles is all,* he thought. *I should make it in less than an hour even with the uneven terrain.*

But he was slowing down.

Maybe two hours.

Pederson sat off to one side of the trail, his head down. *How long have I been sitting here?* he wondered. *Maybe it will take three hours to get home.*

And then, unbidden, came the thought, *Maybe I'll never get home.*

Big Stanford engineer brain; Silicon Valley Master of the Universe. Forgetting water. What any dumb cow would have thought of first.

The pig probably did him a favor.

Pederson's thinking had been confused for a while. He wasn't even sure he was heading in the right direction anymore. He found himself sitting in the dirt as often as he found himself stumbling around.

A single, threatening grunt and his brain instantly focused. He saw that the sun had descended closer to the horizon. It was past noon.

He stood up, nocking the arrow with shaking hands. Where

had the grunt come from? Then the pig did him another favor. It grunted again, just ahead of him on the trail.

The pigs came around a curve in the trail and stopped, seemingly as surprised to see him as he was to see them. There were four of them, but only one of them mattered.

Pederson recognized Himmler. One of the smart ones. One of the mutants, the one with the prissy little mustache. The javelina examined him, his eyes taking in the bow as if he understood what it was. He grunted, and the other pigs moved forward, surrounding Himmler, giving him cover and depriving Pederson of a clear shot.

Himmler gave another grunt, which sounded to Pederson's ears very much like a command, and the three pigs started forward. But Pederson ignored them. He was likely to get only one shot off, maybe two if he was lucky. He wasn't going to be able to kill them all.

But he had a hunch that he didn't have to kill them all. He only had to kill Himmler; the others would be just pigs, afraid of men, mostly harmless.

When his three attackers had covered half the distance between them, Pederson finally had a shot. Himmler sensed what was happening and turned to run, but in doing so, he turned sideways. Pederson had been aiming for the chest and was going to miss by a foot to the left, but by turning broadside, Himmler had made himself a bigger target.

The arrow thudded into his neck.

The pig squealed, and his scent glands released, filling the clearing with the stink of death. He thrashed, turning over and over again, which only drove the arrow deeper. Then, instead of slowly subsiding, he simply stopped in mid-motion and collapsed.

The other three pigs had turned around. They looked around as if confused, saw Pederson pulling a second arrow out of his quiver, and turned to run.

Pederson released the second arrow, knowing he'd probably miss but angry enough to try anyway. To his amazement, he caught a retreating pig in the rear end, and it tumbled head over heels and lay still.

One less to worry about, Pederson thought.

He couldn't dislodge the arrow from Himmler. It had apparently embedded itself in bone. He was able to draw the arrow out of the soft tissue of the second dead pig though.

He went on, his thirst forgotten for a moment, feeling pretty good about himself. The mighty hunter.

That feeling only lasted until the next curve in the trail. Waiting for him were another dozen pigs, and standing thirty feet back was a single pig who regarded him with calculating eyes. This one had hair hanging down past his mouth, like a Fu Manchu mustache.

Genghis, Pederson thought.

Then he thought, *Shit*.

He raised his bow, knowing it was hopeless.

The javelinas must have heard the whine of the motorcycle first because they started milling about in panic despite the commanding grunts of the mutant pig.

Then Pederson heard it too. The motorcycle went whizzing past Genghis, bowled over a couple of the smaller javelinas, roared up to Pederson's side, and stopped. The rider grinned at Pederson, and through the dirt and grime, he recognized Barry Hunter.

"Hop on, neighbor," the man said.

Pederson had never been so happy to see another person. He put the arrow back in the quiver and climbed on behind his rescuer, holding the bow with one hand and grabbing Hunter around the waist with the other.

The motorcycle accelerated away, weaving dangerously for few moments, almost giving the javelinas a chance to catch them. Then the pigs were left behind, obscured by a cloud of dust.

Chapter Twenty-Two

B arbara woke up with the sun in her eyes. She'd gone to sleep without closing the curtains like she normally did.

Why'd I do that? she wondered. *Did I hit the sauce last night?*

A bolt of pain up her leg brutally reminded her of what had happened. She groaned and rolled out of bed. She tested her footing. The leg was swollen. She could feel the pounding of her pulse in the injured leg, and it was painful, but she used the trick she had learned of pretending the pain was happening to someone else and stood up.

She fell back into bed with a cry.

She immediately pushed herself up and tried again. This time, she stayed standing.

If rampaging swine hadn't been surrounding her house, Barbara probably would have allowed herself some bed rest. But these were no ordinary pigs. She'd seen that look in the smart one's eyes. The Mean One. Unless she missed her guess, he was probably trying to figure out how to get in.

She made it to the bathroom and took a pain pill—only one because she wanted to be alert.

It was time for her to figure out what her vulnerabilities were.

She hobbled into the living room and saw giant cracks in her window. She had an old, plate-glass window; they were illegal now, but it seemed to her the plate glass was clearer than shatter glass, and she'd connived to get one installed. No one could get around the law better than a career law enforcement officer; no doubt that was why some of them became corrupt. But Barbara's ethical failures were small ones, petty ones.

One more blow—however they'd managed that—and that window was going down. She went to the garage and started hauling scrap lumber into the living room. She had just enough to cover the picture window, but that wouldn't take care of the smaller windows.

She pulled one of her picture frames off of the wall. The backing was plastic. Strong enough to hold out for a short time. Better than nothing.

Barbara got to work. The more she hobbled about, the more functional her leg became. She'd no doubt pay the price tonight, but it needed to be done.

By the time she was finished, her house looked half-empty. Much of the wooden furniture had been broken apart. The pictures on the walls had been sacrificed, as had the bookshelves. It looked like the inside of the house had exploded and attached itself to the walls and windows, but it looked pretty secure to her. The little monsters would probably be able to get in eventually, but not all at once, and she still had thirty-six bullets.

Barbara went to the closet and pulled out her leather jacket. The electricity had gone off during the night, but despite the sweltering heat, she put the jacket on. Then, as long as she was being silly, she pinned on her old badge in its old spot.

Now, she was ready.

She poured herself a stiff drink and sat down and waited.

A crash woke Barbara up. It had come from the bedroom.

She went over to the magnetic knife rack in the kitchen and picked up the biggest knife she had.

A pig had managed to get its head through one of the wooden slats she'd nailed across the window. It was squealing, unable to get in or out. She examined it for a few moments. Just a pig, one of the dumb ones. She ran the blade across its throat, and the squealing grew muted, and then there was silence. Barbara left the pig hanging there.

"Next?" she called out. "Which one of you bastards wants it next? How about your leader? Is he too much of a coward?"

I'm off my rocker, she thought. It wasn't the danger that was making her feel alive. No, it was the loneliness. That's why she was having a conversation with pigs.

"Come and get it, you little bastards. Come on!"

There was a thump in the living room, and she turned and strode purposefully toward the sound. A smaller pig had squeezed through a gap, and a bigger pig was trying to get in.

She drew her gun and shot the one running around the living room. Then she walked over and slit the throat of the bigger one. She left that one hanging there too.

That's one way to fill the gaps, she thought and giggled.

Yep, completely off my rocker.

And then they were trying to come in from every direction, and she was too busy to giggle or tell herself she was nuts. Too busy killing.

By nightfall, Barbara was covered with blood. Almost too late, it occurred to her that she had no light. She managed to find time between battles to search for her old Maglite. She found it with the rest of her sheriff stuff in the closet. It still had strong batteries, and its heft was reassuring. She'd never actually had to wield it in action, and she had always been curious about how it would perform. She slammed it into the next intruder. It connected with a satisfying thud, and it still shone brightly.

Not bad, Barbara thought. She chuckled, and that's when she knew the frequency of attacks was diminishing. She was finding time for thought, for humor. She found some candles and lit them in every room, keeping them well away from the walls. She always had the makings of a fire in the fireplace though she almost never lit it even on the coldest winter nights, which, by Crook County standards, weren't cold at all. She hated cleaning up afterward, but she liked the look and smell of a wood fire.

She took some papers off the table and set them on fire. Wait, wasn't that her driver's license renewal? Oh well. She'd be lucky to be alive, much less driving around, after this.

The fire was soon roaring, and it was atavistically satisfying. The attacks came less and less frequently, almost as if good, old-fashioned fire was driving the pigs away. Barbara checked her watch and was astonished to find that both the day and the following night were almost over. She'd been besieged for almost a full day.

Boar heads stuck out of every wall as if she was some kind of mad great white hunter.

"Bwana," she said out loud.

She heard a scream from outside. It sounded like the most pissed-off animal she'd ever heard. It was also surprisingly human-sounding.

And somehow, she knew she'd won, that the enemy was giving up, that the leader's dumber followers were defying him.

Barbara checked her ammo.

She still had five bullets.

Chapter Twenty-Three

Peggy knew more about what was going on than Mark even though she hadn't left the building all day.

They'd starting getting reports in the grocery store early in the morning that there were rampaging pigs terrorizing the area, she told him. They'd turned on the radio, not believing it despite the continuing reports. Peggy had tried calling Mark to tell him about the joke, she said, but cellphone service had died at around the same time. Not much later, a customer had come in to say that the one cellphone tower in town had toppled over.

"Gophers," the customer had said knowingly, and they had laughed at the absurdity of it.

They'd laughed about it, that is, until a customer had come in bleeding from the thigh. The tusks of the pig that had attacked her had hit her femoral artery, and the old woman had bled out right there in the produce aisle of the grocery store.

They'd closed for business after that but had kept the doors unlocked in case anyone needed shelter.

"I tried to talk Justin and Brian into staying," Peggy told Mark, sounding worried. "They wanted to get home to their girlfriends. I hope they made it."

Mark hugged her and didn't tell her what he thought. Without a .30-06, he doubted they had made it very far. "What about Mrs. Andrews?" he asked.

"She didn't show up for work."

Again, Mark held this tongue. Both of them knew how unusual that was. In fact, Mark didn't think that anything less than the end of the world would keep that woman from showing up for work, which meant the end of the world had indeed arrived.

About that time, they heard crashing down below them.

"Someone's in the store," Peggy whispered.

Mark was pretty sure what was in the store. He looked around the apartment. It was fairly sparse. They hadn't been able to bring much with them from Idaho, so they'd scrounged from friends and relatives. Their place was furnished with castoffs, like what Mark imagined a hippie apartment must have looked like in the '60s: a wooden wire spool table, a broken-down lawn chair, and a black-and-white TV, probably the last one in the entire country. "We ought to sell it on eBay as an antique," he'd joked. "Perfect for Humphrey Bogart movies."

There were a couple of solid pieces like a nice table Peggy's mom had given them. Four nice chairs. A sofa that wasn't too disgusting.

"Help me out," he said, dragging the sofa to the door. She didn't question him, just set her slender little body to pushing while he dragged. They got it to the top of the stairs and let go. It slid, rattling, down the steps and banged into the door.

"That's good start," Mark said.

"Not the table!" Peggy exclaimed when he went over to it.

"The wire spool," he said, turning at the last second as though that had always been his plan. She willingly helped him roll it out the door and pushed it onto the sofa below, where it landed with a crash.

By the time they finished, all that was left in the apartment was their bed, the nice table and chairs, and the refrigerator, which was too heavy to move.

"What more do we need?" Peggy asked.

Food? Mark wanted to say. *More ammo?*

She hugged him, and suddenly, her body was racked with sobs. "They're dead, aren't they?" she sobbed.

Mark didn't answer. He'd only told her that he'd been chased by javelinas. He hadn't told her what a close call it had been. But she'd managed to intuit it anyway.

"We're safe now," he said after a while. "Unless the damn pigs have ladders."

They lay in bed, feeling like the last people on Earth. Most of the area's residents lived outside of town. There was a motel at the edge of downtown, but it was pretty much the abode of the near-homeless, who spent most of their paychecks in weekly installments for lodging.

Mark hugged the girl he knew he'd spend the rest of his life with. She was skinny with small but delectable breasts and an incredibly thin waist. When she put on full makeup, she was as pretty as a model, and indeed, she'd been approached by scouts. She'd laughed it off, certain they were just dirty old men, but Mark wasn't so sure.

Peggy loved art. She loved comics and *Doctor Who* and *Adventure Time* as much as he did. He had never imagined that was possible: a beautiful girl with a kind heart who loved *Doctor Who*. It had seemed very unlikely.

So he'd waited for the dark side to emerge. Or the phoniness.

But she was exactly as she appeared on the surface. Only deeper.

Mark envisioned a nice, middle-class life: buying a house, working until they were sixty-five, maybe returning to Moscow someday. Maybe someday, he'd have time to work on his art. A nice, modest life.

Without pigs. Just the normal deer and bears and such. Wild pigs seemed un-American somehow.

Peggy snuggled up to him in that way that he knew would lead to the next thing, and he ran his hand down to the indentation above her ass, which she knew would lead to the next thing, and the next thing *did* lead to the next thing, and then they fell asleep in each other's arms, spent.

Chapter Twenty-Four

The old man on the back of the motorcycle was hanging on tight to Barry. He shouted directions in Barry's ear, and Barry decided to follow them. They ended up at a huge barn, which was covered by nailed-on wooden planks. It was by far the most secure structure from swarming javelinas that Barry had yet seen. He had a feeling this old man knew what he was doing.

Pederson got off the bike, opened one of the swinging doors at the front of the barn, and motioned Barry in. He drove into the darkness, and while he was parking, the overhead lights came on: fluorescent lights as bright as the ones in a mall store.

"Pederson," his host said, walking over and sticking out his grimy hand.

Barry grabbed it and shook it hard. "We've met, actually. At one of the county commission meetings. You wanted to close the borders of the county and shoot all trespassers, or something like that."

Fortunately for Barry, his host laughed. "I wouldn't mind that at all. But what I was arguing for was no more subdivisions. Enough is enough. We have no water. None. It's all shipped in from outside. How long can that last? How long before some disaster shuts off the water supply?"

"Now?" Barry ventured. "I think the disaster is happening now."

"I wouldn't put it past the skunk pigs," Pederson said. He looked thoughtful for a moment then nodded. "All Razorback has to do is break the pipes at the Hermiston Dam. Hell, if I can figure it out, he surely can."

His words added to the urgency Barry felt. He'd left Jenny and probably Aragorn with only a bathtub of water to rely on if the bathroom spigot stopped flowing. Barry knew that humans could go for a lot longer without food than most people would suspect, but they couldn't go very long without water.

"I've got to get going," he said.

"Wait, Barry. Are you armed?"

He stopped in mid-stride. "No. I'm not sure I even know how to use a gun."

"Come along." Pederson walked over to a locked cabinet on one side of the barn. Barry looked around. It was pretty clear to him that Pederson spent most of his time here instead of at his house—and not only now because it was safer but even before the recent crisis. There was a workbench that took up a large part of the back of the barn, and on it were intricate objects that looked very high-tech. These weren't mere gadgets, Barry suspected, but things probably very few people would understand only a few feet from moldering hay bales, which Barry was beginning to believe were there more for show than anything else.

The cabinet was full of weapons: rifles, shotguns, revolvers, and pistols.

Pederson pulled out a high-tech-looking pistol and checked the clip then slid it back home. He handed the gun to Barry. "Three shots left. Careful; the safety is off. That's this little button right here. Now, ordinarily, you want to keep the safety on. But don't forget to take it off when you need to, all right?"

Barry nodded. The pistol felt comfortable in his hand.

"First rule," said Pederson, "is never point a gun at another person unless you mean to use it."

"Which means never point a gun at another person," Barry said.

"Exactly," Pederson seemed pleased with his answer. "Now, I have a little target range over here. It's only twenty feet long, but I doubt you'll ever have to shoot farther than that. So just lift the barrel up like it's an extension of your hand and pull the trigger slowly. Don't jerk it."

Barry raised the gun, aimed it at the target, and fired. The gunshot was deafening.

Pederson laughed and patted him on the back. "Not bad. You only missed by the side of a barn."

Barry grumbled a little and tried again. This time, he saw the target sway from the passage of the bullet.

"Try one more time," Pederson said.

Barry was starting to get a sense of it. He fired again, and the third time was the charm. He hit the outer circle of the target.

"You're a natural," Pederson said. He took the gun from Barry's hand, pulled another clip out of his back pocket, and swapped it for the spent one. Barry noticed he put on the safety before he handed the gun back.

"You've got fifteen bullets in that clip," Pederson informed him. "I'll give you another clip before you leave. With any luck, you'll make it home. But before you leave, we need to talk."

Pederson sat on an upturned milk can. There was another open one a few feet away. Barry went to reach for it, but Pederson waved him off. "That's my spittoon," he said, proving it by shooting a stream of tobacco juice out of his mouth. "Sit on one of the hay bales," he said, motioning to the stack behind Barry. "They're softer anyway."

Barry pulled out a bale and hauled it over to where the old man was sitting. He thought of Pederson as an old man even though by most lights, he was an old man himself. But somehow, Pederson was an *old* old man.

"Where are the authorities?" Barry asked. "Where are the cops, the FBI, the fucking National Guard? Don't they know what's happening? Isn't the outside world alarmed at the lack of communication from us?"

"Of course they've noticed, but we're damned isolated. It might take a day or two of fussing around before they do much, depending on who's in charge and how competent he or she is, which is a crapshoot these days.

"Oh, they're responding about as fast as bureaucracy can react when they don't know what the problem is," Pederson continued. "But see, so far, they've sent in a single FBI agent, who was eaten the first time he got out of his car to take a leak. And then they sent in a car full of state troopers, who got as far as town before they were surrounded in the park and taken out.

They killed, oh, I don't know…fifty of the damn pigs, but that's nothing to the Leader."

"Razorback?"

"Yeah…Razorback. Good name. Well, the javelinas have been overpopulating for years but somehow managed to keep it hidden. There are a lot more than anyone could possibly have conceived of. I figure there was a whole litter of the mutant ones…Razorback's offspring. I've named a few of them. There is one that looks like he has a Fu Manchu mustache."

"I've met him."

"I call him Genghis. Another one with a small mustache I call Himmler. The others I haven't gotten a close enough look at to name. They seem to have some kind of control over the others…" His voice drifted off, then he said, "These aren't skunk pigs or javelinas or whatever you want to call them. These here are a new animal. I call them Tuskers on account of their larger tusks. But their tusks aren't the only thing that's bigger."

"Their brains," Barry said.

"They're fucking geniuses: for pigs at least. All of them swine Einsteins."

The old man got Barry thinking. He'd had the glimmer of a plan for a while, and now, he gave voice to it. "I wonder…if we kill Razorback, maybe the rest of them will give up."

Pederson nodded. "Not bad. But I'm pretty sure his offspring would take over. But you're right; without the Tuskers, the other pigs are just javelinas. Annoying but not particularly dangerous."

"Hamilton never said anything about *any* of this."

Pederson leaned over and spit tobacco juice into the milk can. "Hamilton was a good man for all his anger issues, but he was by the book. Turns out Razorback was smarter than he was. Besides, he wouldn't listen to me. I've been telling him for years that he was undercounting the skunk pigs. By the way, his van is parked on top of Canner's Butte. No sign of him. Not so much as a bone. One thing about these pigs, they let nothing go to waste."

"How do you know all this?"

"Ham radio and a generator. Keeps working when everything else fails. We had a pretty good network going locally. Except…Johnson and Emerson have stopped calling or responding, which leaves only me in the north part of the county and Hawkins in the south and nothing in between. I've sent messages out to some of my buddies out of state, but frankly, I don't think they believe me. Don't blame them."

Pederson stood up and dropped the entire wad of chaw into the milk can. He turned, wiping his chin. "So…I can't help you much about where to go."

"What about town? Surely they have enough firepower there to hold them off."

"*Had*, past tense. Sure, if they had known the pigs were coming, they might have been all right. But Razorback caught them with their pants down."

"Are you sure?"

Pederson eyed Barry speculatively. He hauled out a bag of chew and stuck a plug in his cheek, staring at his guest the whole time. Barry must have passed muster because Pederson stood up and gestured for Barry to follow him.

There was a spiral staircase near the center of the barn. It was gorgeous with black enamel paint and golden scrollwork along the sides. The lettering looked like Latin, probably something that had meaning for Pederson. Barry was figuring out that this was no hick farmer. There was a razor-sharp brain behind his folksy ways. Not to mention, Barry knew enough about farming to know that all the equipment in the barn was first-rate, top-of-the-line, and that this little valley didn't produce enough for most local farmers to afford that kind of equipment.

The old man had a viewing platform like the one at the top of a lighthouse. From there, they could see the whole valley, including the town. There was smoke coming from several places in town, and Barry could see fires still burning.

"Where do I go for help?" he asked. "Doesn't the town have some kind of emergency communications?"

"I hate to tell you, Barry, but the Internet *is* the emergency communication. That's what it was designed for. But it turns out that when everything is transmitted on wires or fiber optic cables or from towers, and when they are dug up or toppled, we're pretty vulnerable."

Barry couldn't keep the frustration out of his voice. "We can't just do *nothing*. Where do I go for help?"

"Hell if I know," the old man said, leaning over and spitting. He missed the milk can but didn't seem too concerned about it. "Me? I'm sticking around here. Won't let myself get caught like that again. Eventually, the outside world will cotton on to what's happening. We just have to survive until then."

After everything Barry had just heard, he trusted complacency even less than before. He was surprised that Pederson had that attitude. But when he looked into his host's eyes, he realized Pederson didn't really believe what he was saying. His eyes were crinkled up with humor. "Hell, I'm too old to move," Pederson said. "Gonna die one way or another, and I'd rather it be at home. Though when it comes to it, I'd rather not be pig shit. I'll find some way to keep that from happening."

"I'm going to see if I can find anyone in town," Barry said, getting to his feet.

"You might also check out Barbara Weiss' house. She's not far away, on Bradford Court. You know where that is?"

Barry nodded.

"Good. She was a sheriff for twenty years. A tough, competent lady. Be careful; she's probably armed. In fact, I guarantee it. And she probably won't be shy about shooting anything that moves."

Barry nodded. "I'll try that."

"You do that."

Barry extended his hand. "Good luck, Pederson."

"You too, young man," Pederson said, looking solemn. He couldn't have been more than ten years older than Barry, but Barry knew what he meant.

Bart Hoskins had been pretty shocked when he'd found his cat's body and even more shocked when his Labrador had disappeared from the backyard. After meeting with Peter Gandry, he'd gone home to change his shirt because he'd spilled egg on it while eating breakfast. But he was so unsettled that he decided to take the rest of the day off. His wife was visiting her mother, and the house was pleasingly quiet. No *Judge Judy* blaring from the TV all afternoon.

The next morning, he'd called in sick.

He sat reading a book in peace until his neighbor started mowing his lawn. Bart put down the book and sighed. He contemplated using some earplugs. The sound of lawn mowers was the sound Bart hated most. It was his screeching chalkboard sound, his kazoo, the thing that drove him up the wall.

After a while, Bart realized the dreadful sound wasn't going up or down or nearer or farther; it was just roaring away at the same annoying pitch. He opened the back door, propped himself on the bottom rail of his fence, and poked his head over it, and there was the mower, rattling away in the middle of the half-mowed lawn, but no Jerry.

Bart went back into the house just in time to hear the doorbell. He hurried to the door to find Lyle Pederson walking away; he'd almost reached his huge, black pickup.

"I'm here, Lyle!" Bart called out.

Pederson looked annoyed. He turned around, walked back to the house, and went inside, shoving some papers in Bart's hands as he went by. "I need you to notarize these," he said.

Bart spread them out on the table and started reading then looked up sharply. "Are they your relatives?"

"None of your business."

Bart flushed. That was true; it was just that, as a respected banker in a small town, he wasn't used to being talked to that way. "I'll be glad to notarize these, but we need a witness."

"Who's your neighbor? The one not mowing the lawn?"

"Jerry Harper?"

Pederson grabbed the papers and signed "Jerry Harper" on the witness line.

"But…"

"Listen, Hoskins. I doubt Mr. Harper is ever going to dispute this. Just go with it, okay? I'll make it worth your while. You've been wanting some of my land—I'll sell you ten acres. How's that?"

Bart got up, went to his office, and returned with a notary stamp, which he slammed onto the papers, and then he signed his own name. "Anything else, Lyle?"

"Yeah, if you don't mind, don't tell anyone else about my financial condition. I got a call from Peter Gandry today. I want you to tell him to shove it."

Bart was speechless at first, then he sputtered, "I assure you, Mr. Pederson..."

"Don't worry about it," the old man said, not sounding that upset. "I realize what a temptation it is for you. But no more, you hear?"

"Yes, sir," Bart said.

Pederson got up. "Don't bother to show me out," he said and headed for the door. At the last second, he turned around. "Oh, one other thing, Hoskins. If I were you, I'd stay inside for the next few days. I'd kind of like it if you'd survive all this."

He slammed the door behind him.

Bart found himself shaking from the conversation.

Survive?

He'd gone from calling the old man "Lyle" to "Mr. Pederson" to "Sir" in one short conversation.

It was disturbing how fast he'd descended from an important banker to the scared little man he really was.

Chapter Twenty-Five

Mark and Peggy were safe, all right. But they were also hungry and thirsty. The water had stopped flowing sometime during the night. Everything in the refrigerator was starting to spoil. The smell was getting so bad, they'd taken the garbage out onto the deck and dumped it into the street.

That may have been a mistake because that only attracted the javelinas, who rooted and grunted outside their window all morning. Occasionally, one would look up at them with what seemed to Mark to be an evil gleam in its eyes.

The loft was all one big room with a small alcove for the toilet and shower. Windows ran along the entire length of the street side. The space had probably been an office in an earlier incarnation. There was a small door in one corner that led out onto the roof of the grocery store's terrace. It was a great perk when the temperature wasn't too hot to enjoy it.

From this vantage point, they could see the entire main street. Mark spent the morning sitting in the beat-up old chair that a previous tenant had left behind and that was left out, rain or shine. It was disgusting and moldy, but he didn't care anymore. He just wanted to see someone moving about.

Anyone.

But the streets were abandoned, like in an old Western when the bad guys were headed for town and everyone was hiding.

Which is exactly what's happening, Mark thought.

All that was needed to complete the picture were some tumbleweeds. Right on cue, some sagebrush tumbled down the street, followed by a dust devil.

Mark whistled the spaghetti Western tune, but it wasn't as

funny as he thought it would be. In fact, it made him shiver. He looked up at the sky. It might have been a sunny day, but there was so much smoke in the air, he couldn't tell. The fires had burned out overnight, but Broadway, the second most important street in town outside of Main Street (yes, the people here actually called their main street Main Street), was gutted. He coughed. The smoke had been tickling the back of his throat all morning, and his eyes were red. But he'd wanted to see what was happening outside.

He went back into the apartment. Peggy was at the counter, separating out the food that could be saved from the food that needed to be tossed. None of it had much moisture content.

He licked his dry lips. Hadn't he read somewhere to put a pebble in your mouth when there was no water? He glanced around the apartment for something pebble-y then abandoned the idea. With his luck, he'd choke on the damn thing.

They'd both used the toilet that morning, and even if they hadn't been so thirsty, the stink was enough to make him long for water to use for flushing.

As he stomped around the room, the floor creaked and gave way a little. Mark had often wondered if their bed would end up on top of the cereal aisle in the grocery store someday.

Which gave him an idea.

"We got any of our mountain climbing gear around?" he asked Peggy. "Or is it in storage?"

She didn't look up from her sorting. "I think we just threw it in the closet last time."

The two had decided to take up an outdoor activity, and they had decided on rock climbing. They'd done it only twice. The first time, Peggy had sort of freaked out. Mark had teased her about it, but the second time, he'd freaked out even worse. They had almost called for help to get him down, but he'd finally summoned the courage to complete the climb.

But now he remembered that, when they'd come back, they'd tossed the gear onto the floor of the closet under the mostly unused coats and sweaters they'd brought south with them.

Mark rooted around the closet and found the ice axe. They

hadn't known what they were doing and had ordered mountain climbing kits instead of rock climbing kits. They'd naively thought it wouldn't matter.

Nothing more useless than an ice axe in this part of the country. The axe was sharp, unused. He grabbed it and swung it to test its heft. *Yeah, that oughta do it.*

He stomped around the loft some more, and Peggy finally turned away from what she was doing and watched him curiously. There was a particular spot that he avoided because it made so much noise when he walked on it and because…well, it really did feel pretty shaky.

He got down on his knees and used the axe to pry up the floorboards. Underneath were some old wires that he was pretty sure weren't active anymore even when the electricity was on. Even if they were, it was safe enough now. He sliced through the wires, wondering if he was guaranteeing a fire when the power came back.

But he was thirsty. Really, really thirsty. Mark didn't think he'd ever been so thirsty in his life. It had just never come up. There had always been fluids around no matter where he went. Even the longest stretch of desert highway had gas stations with soda machines.

There was old particle board beneath the wires, and Mark quickly punched a hole in that, raining dust and fragments all over the canned foods directly below. The cans were so close he could almost reach out and grab them.

"Bring me a rope, sweetie," he said, hacking away industriously.

The supporting beams were twelve inches apart. He thought he could probably squeeze through, but it would be tight. Peggy could get through easily, but he wasn't going to send her down there without him along.

The reason for the creaking was apparent once he'd removed all the junk in between. One of beams was rotted half through. Mark took a swing at it with the axe, and the blade sliced through the soft wood like butter. He cut the rest of the wood away, creating a nice, two-foot-wide hole.

"I hope the whole floor doesn't give way," Peggy said

doubtfully. She was carrying a coiled rope. "Mrs. Andrews is going to be so pissed."

I hope so, Mark thought. *I hope she's alive to be pissed.* "Better than finding our mummified bodies," he said aloud.

"Ha, ha."

"Don't worry; there are safety redundancies built into structures like this," Mark said confidently. He knew no such thing, but it sounded good. Now that he was finished, he didn't think he'd need the rope at all. He lowered himself into the hole and felt around with his feet. His toes grazed the cans on top of one of the shelves, and some of them tumbled onto the floor.

"What if those pigs are down there?" Peggy asked worriedly.

Thanks for the image, Mark almost said. His feet were dangling down, and he suddenly had a squirmy feeling in his chest, like when he was swimming in a lake and wondered about the nasty creatures in the depths. "I'm sure we would have heard them," he said. His voice was steady, which kind of surprised him. In fact, his calmness through this whole ordeal was surprising him. He'd always figured when the zombie apocalypse came, he'd be one of those idiots who ran around screaming until they were dragged down and eaten.

I guess you never know until it happens, he thought.

Then he decided, *If I hang by my hands, I should easily reach the top shelf.* With a deep breath, he lowered himself the rest of the way. His fingers slipped in the dust, but he managed to hold on.

His knees slammed into the metal shelf, and he raised them until he could feel the cans with his feet again. He knocked more of them off, wincing at the noise, hoping the javelinas outside couldn't hear. When the shelf was clear and his footing seemed solid, he let go of the floor above.

Whoa! Mark teetered to one side, then the other, then caught his balance. The shelf itself was wobbling, and he feared it would topple over, but then it stabilized. He felt for the next shelf down with his foot, sliding the cans to one side, then felt for the next shelf down.

He jumped the final distance to the ground, nearly turning his ankle on one of the rolling cans. But then he was down, on two feet, and looking up into the shining, admiring face of Peggy.

She gave him a thumbs-up.

He answered her in kind. Neither of them wanted to speak, as if it would jinx the whole enterprise or bring the pigs running—which was kind of silly after the clatter he had made.

Almost reluctantly, Mark looked toward the front of the store, fearful of what he'd see. It was only then that he remembered the iron grating that covered the door and windows. Despite her Anglo-Saxon name, Mrs. Andrews was Korean, and she'd moved there from L.A. She'd automatically installed security measures before she understood that she didn't need them.

Well, I'll be damned, Mark thought, relief flooding his body. Unless these pigs could fly or had plasma cutters, Peggy and he were about as safe as they could be. With an entire store full of supplies. They'd hit the apocalypse lottery!

He went into the storage room and started hauling out boxes of food. He used them to create a staircase leading up to the hole in the ceiling. When the last box was in place, he was exhausted, but he marched triumphantly up the makeshift stairs and into the loft.

Peggy was laughing and clapping her hands. "Can I go down there?" she asked.

"Go ahead," he said. "I think we're safe."

He sat back while she "shopped" below: a jar of peaches, a six-pack of bottled water, a loaf of bread, and some peanut butter and jelly. She started to bring up more, but he stopped her.

"We have all the time in the world," he said. "Besides, the authorities should be arriving any time."

She nodded then went to their kitchenette and grabbed some plates and glasses.

They sat on the floor, near the hole, and ate a meal. Peanut butter and jelly had never tasted so good. And plain old bottled water was ambrosia.

Mark was still eating when Peggy sprang up and went to the table. She sat down and started scribbling.

"What are you doing?" he asked.

"I'm making a list of what we're buying," she said. "So I can give it to Mrs. Andrews and we can reimburse her."

Mark stared at her but didn't say anything.

Let her keep the illusion, he thought. *What harm can it do?*

Chapter Twenty-Six

Halfway to town, Barry had a change of heart.

He figured Pederson knew what he was talking about: that the authorities in town, if any, wouldn't be much help. Certainly, the smoke from the still-burning buildings was convincing evidence that no one was in charge down there.

Barry stopped where the entrance to his subdivision met the main highway. There was only one highway in the valley. In fact, it was the only road running through the valley.

When Jenny and Barry had first moved to town, there had been a bank robbery at the little Bank of America branch on Main Street. Barry had walked into Lucille's Diner to find the locals laughing about it.

"What's so funny?" he'd asked.

"There's only one road in and out of this town," old Patterson had said. "Sheriff Butler probably had a roadblock up before the robber left the bank!"

Sure enough, the bank robber had been stopped on the highway within ten minutes.

What Barry was wondering now was why there wasn't any traffic. The town might be isolated, but they still got visitors. There was a nice state park down by the river. They weren't Siberia. And no matter what rational and reasonable explanations Pederson had offered about slow bureaucracies and incompetent officials, Barry couldn't understand why relief hadn't come.

He turned the bike away from town and followed the steep, back-and-forth turns and switchbacks up the canyon. He wasn't even halfway to the top when he saw the rockslide.

More like a mountainslide, Barry thought. It was as if the entire top of the canyon had come off, burying the road under hundreds of feet of dirt and rock. *How did the Tuskers manage that?* he wondered. He knew a lot of these hillsides were barely held together by the thin vegetation, so if they'd eaten it all away, that would explain it.

But what wasn't explainable was how the Tuskers had figured all that out.

Barry had no way of knowing when the landslide had happened, but from the desiccated remains of the pulled-up foliage, he was guessing more than a day, maybe even two days. If so, it would've been about the time everything started to go to hell.

Had this been the trigger?

It explained why no one had showed up to bail them out. Add the necessity for helicopters to the lack of communication, incompetent officials, and slow bureaucracy, and it made sense that help hadn't arrived yet. They were on their own for now.

Barry turned the motorcycle around and headed back to town. Pederson had filled the tank with gas, so he wasn't worried about that. He felt the gun the old man had given him digging into his stomach. It was so strange to be armed: Barry Hunter, the peacenik, toting a gun.

Remember to take off the safety, he told himself. *Point the gun and gently squeeze the trigger.* He repeated the mantra a few more times to himself because he sensed he was going to need it.

He slowed down at the entrance to the subdivision that Barbara Weiss, the former sheriff, lived in. Barry saw a sign that said "Javelina Heights" and snorted at the irony. He'd forgotten that was the name of this benighted development. Only a few houses had been built before the crash.

If he remembered right, Bradford Court was the first street on the right, and Barbara's home was the only one on the cul-de-sac. When Pederson had first mentioned her, it hadn't occurred to Barry that the old man was referring to the same Barbara who showed up at the Bleeding Hearts Club meetings. It wasn't until Pederson gave him the address that he realized it was the same woman. What Barry remembered most about her was that she seemed to be on the hunt for a man, but in their little group, only Patterson was available, and he was in his nineties.

Hard to believe that the femininely dressed and well-coifed liberal had once been a sheriff! She'd kept that juicy bit of information to herself.

She might make a good ally in my searches, Barry thought.

From the corner, he could see down into the town. Broadway was a blackened wasteland. Main Street had somehow managed to avoid the fires, but it looked abandoned. Was there any point in going down there? There on the highway, he could see in all directions. He didn't think the pigs could trap him there. But once he was among the buildings, there could be a trap on any corner.

Just a quick look. Stick to the middle of the street. Get ready to motor out of there. He passed Barbara's subdivision and headed downward.

Barry started coughing before he even reached the first buildings. The smoke hung heavy in the air, and he remembered one of the locals mentioning the atmospheric inversions that the area suffered, especially when the farmers were burning the fields.

His eyes teared up so badly he almost couldn't see. Somewhere, a spark must have touched down on some sage and ignited it; he was terribly allergic to sage.

Coughing and blinking, he drove headlong into the ambush. A dozen pigs lined the road. One of the Tuskers was leading them. He was weaving in and out among his followers as if rallying them to hold firm.

Barry saw daylight on the sidewalk to the left and accelerated toward it. At the last second, one of the javelinas tried to cover the gap, but he bowled it over. He looked in the rearview mirror and saw the Tusker walk up the struggling animal and slash it with his huge tusks. Blood spurted into the air.

Vader, Barry thought. *His name is Vader.*

From that point on, Barry was more careful. He thought

perhaps Vader's crew was there to keep the townspeople from escaping, and he'd caught them off guard. He wasn't sure how he was going to get past them on the way out. But there were bike trails all over the place; generations of children had found ways past the road, and Barry was sure he'd find a path.

He drove down the middle of Main Street since it was widest street and gave him the most space. There was no one in sight, but toward the far end, he heard someone shouting.

"Hey, mister!" a girl called.

Barry was confused at first. Looking around, he couldn't see anyone.

"Up here," came a male voice. Barry stopped the motorcycle and looked up at the roofs and saw a young couple waving at him from atop the grocery store. He'd talked to the girl before; Peggy was her name.

Barry revved up to edge of the sidewalk. "Are you guys all right?"

"We're great!" the boy answered. "We're safe, and we've got plenty of supplies. Hang there just for a sec. We'll let you in!" He disappeared from view while the girl looked down on Barry, beaming.

Like they're on some kind of adventure, Barry thought. *Not aware of the danger.* "I really can't stop," he said. "I was just looking for someone in charge."

Peggy shook her head. "We haven't seen or heard anyone."

"Well, if you guys are safe, I'm going to keep going, okay?"

She looked disappointed but managed to smile and nod. "I'll tell Mark."

He saw motion at the door of the grocery, which had bars across it. Mark was standing there, looking down at a huge set of keys and trying them, one by one, in the lock.

Barry started to wave him off when he heard the sound of grunting.

The pigs were running so hard that they were grunting with every step. Vader was whipping them on, occasionally slashing at a slowpoke, practically goring his own troops.

Barry revved up the motorcycle for his escape, and in his excitement, he overdid it. The engine stalled. The swarm of pigs was only yards away. The door of the grocery swung open, and Mark yelled at him, "Hurry!"

Barry got off the bike and pushed it up the stairs, lifting it over the last steps with more strength than he realized he possessed, and rolled it into the store. Mark tried to slam the door behind him, but one of the pigs managed to get its snout in, and by the time Barry dropped the bike, two more had made headway.

Barry joined Mark at the door.

"When I count to three, push with everything you got!" Barry shouted. "One…two…*three!*"

The pigs squealed at the pressure, and two of them retreated. The third couldn't have escaped if it wanted to. The door had started cutting into its muzzle.

"One…two…three…PUSH!"

The pig's jaw broke in half, and a sloppy piece of meat and one tusk landed with a splat and a click on the floor as the door slammed shut.

Mark was desperately trying to lock it.

"I think we're safe," Barry said dryly. "Unless pigs have figured out how to turn knobs."

Mark ignored him and locked the door anyway.

And who could blame him?

Chapter Twenty-Seven

Barry had to admit he wasn't sorry to be safe if only for a little while. This young couple had truly created a secure and defensible location. Mark proudly showed Barry his staircase made of boxes and welcomed him to their charming little loft. It was full of food and drink from the grocery store below. He saw an itemized list on the table, with the prices next to the items, and almost laughed.

But then, honesty was nothing to laugh at.

Mark had constructed a trapdoor, and Barry wanted to ask him if he thought pigs could fly, but again, he held off. Pigs who could cause landslides; pigs who could plan ambushes. Who knew what else they were capable of?

They fed him a banquet, and he downed three bottles of water. He hadn't realized how famished he was. They insisted he fill a backpack with water and food and anything else he needed. It was a children's backpack, the only brand the store carried. It had a funny-looking creature on it and said *Adventure Time*. Barry had no idea what that was.

For a few moments, he thought about driving straight up into the hills and getting Jenny to ride back with him. They'd wait it out there, have a party. Surely, it wouldn't be long now.

In fact, what was he really accomplishing?

But now that he was in town, he wanted to see if there were any police officers left, anyone who had put together a self-defense force. If there were, they hadn't shown their faces so far. Mark and Patty hadn't seen anyone either.

Barry spotted a rifle in the corner. "You got ammo for that?"

The young man nodded. "Fourteen bullets left."

There was something haunted in the kid's eyes, and Barry realized that he hadn't always been safe and snug in his aerie.

"I need to go," Barry said, standing up.

"Do you really have to?" Peggy asked. "Can't you stay a little longer?"

"My wife is by herself. When I left her, I thought she was safe. But now that I've seen what these Tuskers are capable of, I'm not so sure. I need to get back to her."

She was nodding during the entire explanation. "Go. She needs you. Take whatever you think you can use, anything at all. I'm sure Mrs. Andrews will understand."

"I'll see if the coast is clear," Mark said, walking out onto the deck.

Peggy came over to Barry and gave him a big hug as if he was her favorite uncle. Looking down at her from close up, Barry saw that she was a gorgeous girl who covered it up with goofy clothing and makeup and hair—to go along with the goofy boyfriend, he supposed.

"I'm glad you're safe here," he murmured.

Mark came back in. "There are a few stragglers," he said. "Probably won't get any better. Come on, I'll see you out."

As they climbed down the boxes, Mark grinned at him. "Tuskers? How did you come up with that name?" He coughed, and Barry realized the store was smoky.

"Lyle Pederson calls them that."

"Pederson? Old guy with the scraggly, stained beard?"

"That's him. Don't be fooled; he's one smart man."

"He's the guy who warned me," Mark said. "If he hadn't told me to take that rifle, I'd be dead right now." He coughed again, and Barry joined him.

Mark pulled out the keys and quickly picked the right one this time. "You ready?"

But Barry was having a coughing fit. His eyes were so swollen he could barely see out of them.

"You all right, Barry?" The words were barely out of Mark's mouth before he started coughing just as badly.

Then they both stopped and stared at each other in shock. *I'm probably as slack-jawed as he is*, Barry thought, *same white face and wide eyes.* The smoke spelled their doom.

They heard a thump behind them, and both of them jumped, Barry with a shout.

It was one of the children's backpacks landing on the floor, followed by another one. Peggy followed them down by way of the boxes, a big knife in her mouth, like a pirate.

"They've set fire to the drugstore next door," she said after sliding the knife into a sheath at her belt. She was preternaturally calm, like a person who was scared to death and was using every ounce of her energy to hide it.

"How..." Mark began to ask then seemed to realize how useless the question was. "Looks like we're coming with you, Barry." Then a look of urgency came over the kid's face. "I have to get the .30-ought."

He scrambled up the boxes while Peggy shrugged on one of the packs. "Mark insisted we be ready to leave on a moment's notice," she said. "I thought he was being overly cautious."

"I'm not sure there is such a thing," Barry said ruefully.

Mark came sliding back down, knocking the boxes over as he came. He snagged the other backpack and ran to the door. There were more than a few javelinas outside, and it was only going to get worse.

"Ready?" he shouted and threw the door open without waiting for an answer.

Barry barely had time to start the bike before Mark and Peggy were out the door. He followed them. They were in the middle of the street. The javelinas were surrounding them but not attacking yet. They were probably waiting for orders from a Tusker.

"Get on the bike, Peggy," Mark said, rifle in hand.

"What about you?"

"I've got a gun," he said. "I'll follow."

One of the javelinas had snuck up behind him. Before he'd even consciously decided to act, Barry had the Glock out and was firing. The pig tumbled to one side. Mark raised his weapon and fired at another one.

Peggy got on the bike. Barry was carefully firing, trying to make each bullet count, but more of the skunk pigs were showing up every second. They were getting surrounded. They weren't going to be able to wait much longer.

Mark was firing and loading, firing and loading, but with every pause, the pigs were getting closer. Barry's Glock clicked, empty. Mark fumbled one of the bullets, and it fell into the dirt. It must have been his last one because he dropped to his knees, frantically searching for it.

Then the javelinas were all over him in a swarm. Barry heard a shout, something that sounded like "Peg…" but was cut off.

Suddenly, the back of the bike was lighter, and Peggy was screaming, charging the band of pigs with her knife. It was so unexpected that the animals actually retreated. But that only revealed Mark's bloody face and sightless eyes.

At this, all the fire seemed to go out of the girl. She stumbled then threw herself on top of Mark, dropping the knife.

Meanwhile, Barry was desperately trying to remember where he'd put the other clip, furious with himself for forgetting. He'd rehearsed everything, over and over again, but he hadn't planned for this.

There was a sudden silence except for Peggy's sobbing. A Tusker walked over to her, standing mere inches away, watching her dispassionately.

Vader, Barry thought. The beast didn't have any distinguishing features other than being slightly bigger than the other javelinas. But there was something about its bearing and the cold-blooded look in its eyes.

Barry found the clip and slipped it into the gun. He raised the Glock and fired at Vader, but one of the Tusker's followers jumped into the path of the bullet. Vader looked at Barry almost contemptuously then looked back at Peggy.

Then the entire pack, dozens of them, swarmed over the girl. She went down without a cry. Barry took another shot at Vader and another and missed both times. The Tusker grunted orders, and half the animals turned and charged Barry.

He stuck the gun in his belt and stared back at Vader to show that he could be just as cold-blooded.

He waited until the pigs were only a couple of feet away before roaring off.

Chapter Twenty-Eight

Barry pounded on the handlebars so hard, he almost fell off the bike. When he reached the grassy median at the edge of town, he stopped and got off, letting the bike fall on its side. He fell to his knees, put his hands to his face, and wept.

He hadn't known those kids for even a day, but he wept as if they were the kids he'd never had. He'd been so happy for them, happy that they had found a safe place. They'd looked so much like he and Jenny had looked when they were first married: picking up on each other's every little need, smiling secret smiles.

When he was cried out, he stood and checked his clip. He had six bullets left. Enough to get home maybe.

That's all he wanted to do. Get home to Jenny. He didn't care about anything else anymore. There was no safe place. There was no way to defeat these creatures. Eventually, rescue would come. They just had to survive until then.

He got back on the bike, noticing as he did so that some of the gas had spilled out. He didn't even check to see how much was left. There would either be enough or there wouldn't.

But when Barry reached the corner of Javelina Heights, he hesitated. He could keep going, hide out in his house, and wait for rescue. But…Pederson had told him to check in on Barbara Weiss. He didn't expect any help from her. That was a lost cause. But he was concerned for her welfare. She was one of the few people he knew down here in Arizona. She'd always seemed like a nice lady.

So, much to his own surprise, he found himself driving into the subdivision and turning onto Bradford Court.

Barry couldn't believe what he was seeing. Starting at the corner, there were dead pigs everywhere, piled up all around the house. It looked like the Alamo, like that movie *Zulu*, like Custer's Last Stand, like…he didn't know what. No one could have survived such an onslaught.

But as Barry drove up, he didn't see any breaches in the defenses.

He turned off the motor, remembering Pederson's warning that Barbara might shoot anything that moved. But he didn't need the warning. It was pretty clear she could take care of herself.

"Hello?" he shouted. "Barbara? It's Barry Hunter."

The door creaked open. A creature out of a nightmare emerged, a stocky, menacing creature, covered from head to toe in blood. Then Barry saw the calm blue eyes within the red paint and heard Barbara's pleasantly low voice as if she was welcoming him for tea.

"Hello, Barry. Nice to see you."

The inside of the house was, if anything, worse. The heads of animals that had tried to get in were mounted on the walls like trophies. Others were lying randomly around the floor. There was a fire burning in the fireplace, but there wasn't a single stick of furniture left in the house. Flies were buzzing about in swarms and following Barbara around as if she was their goddess. She didn't seem to notice.

Barry checked the bathroom. There was a filthy pool of water in the bathtub, but it was cleaner than Barbara was.

"I'm sorry I don't have anything to offer you," she said, traipsing into the kitchen and opening cabinets.

"Why don't you go take a bath?" he suggested. "I'll find something to eat."

Barbara looked down at herself and fingered the leather jacket she was wearing. Barry could barely see the gleam of a gold badge on the front. "Oh, dear. I'm a mess, aren't I? Please forgive me. I won't take long."

She walked into the bathroom and closed the door. He checked the closets in her bedroom and found some frilly pastel dresses but only one pair of pants. He took the trousers, some underwear, and a sensible blouse and laid them outside the bathroom door.

"There's some fresh clothes for you out here," he said, tapping lightly on the door. He heard splashing within and a tuneless humming.

It was the humming that finally got to Barry. He didn't think Barbara was quite right in the head. Something inside her had been knocked off kilter. And who could blame her? It looked like she had fought a battle for the ages.

He managed to wipe off the kitchen table and chairs enough so that they weren't disgusting at least. He got some clean plates from the cupboards, which had managed to avoid the blood and gore. The food and water came out of the backpack that Peggy had given him.

He teared up at that thought and put his head in his hands. He was still grieving when Barbara entered the room.

She had her hair pulled back in a ponytail and was wearing minimal makeup. Her clothes were the plain, functional ones he'd left for her, and she'd found some low-heeled shoes. She looked like a different woman, and Barry had the sudden insight that this was the way she had always looked before she came down to Arizona to search for a man.

Barry thought he preferred this version—or would have if it weren't for that eerily calm demeanor.

"I'm so glad you found something to eat," Barbara said, not seeming to recognize that it wasn't her own food. She sat down, put both elbows on the table, and started eating. She started off daintily, but after she took a few bites, her hunger took over, and she started cramming the sandwiches into her mouth.

"I want you to come with me, Barbara," Barry said when she was finished.

"Oh, I couldn't impose."

"No, you'd be doing me a favor. Me and Jenny, we could use someone who is…handy with a gun."

"I've got five bullets left," she said bluntly.

"Well…you know what I mean," he said. "We need to stick together, to help each other out."

"I can't get ahold of my daughter, Sarah," she said. "She isn't answering."

"None of the phones work, Barbara," he said gently.

She wasn't listening. For the first time, there was crack in her calm exterior. She looked completely desolate for a moment, then the blank expression returned. "She's a busy woman."

Barry got up from the table and started packing up the leftovers. He hoped he wasn't making a mistake, inviting a crazy woman into his home. He looked around at the gore and almost gagged. It didn't matter. He couldn't leave her here.

She followed him docilely out to the motorbike. Then, for the first time, Barry saw a rational thought flicker across her face.

"I have a car," she said. "It's in the garage. They haven't got to it."

He hesitated. It was very tempting. But…he'd seen that cars were vulnerable. And he wouldn't put it past the creatures to have set up roadblocks. With a motorcycle, they could avoid them, head over fields and dells if necessary.

"Do you mind if I siphon some gas?" he asked.

They found some tubing in the garage and quickly filled the bike's tank. A great pressure lifted off Barry, and he realized that he'd been more worried than he'd let on. Every second he'd been on the bike, he'd expected it to run out of gas.

During this whole time, not a single javelina had come into view. Barry thought this was the longest time he'd gone without sighting one. He muttered something out loud to that effect.

"They won't come back," Barbara said. "I *beat* them."

A chill went down his spine. He didn't know if that was true, but it was clear that she believed it.

He gazed at the piles of pigs and thought, *Yeah, this may have been a victory. But not one I'd like to replicate.*

"Hop on, Barbara," he said.

She got on, and the bike immediately sank. Compared to scrawny old Pederson and skinny little Peggy, Barbara was a solid chunk of weight. He surreptitiously checked the tires, and though they were a little flatter, they were holding up.

"Ready?" he asked. He checked to see that she was holding

on and was a little surprised to see that she had her gun in one hand.

They started off, and though the bike was a bit sluggish, it had plenty of power once he got used to compensating for the extra weight.

It was a straight shot for home, and Barry didn't intend to let anything get in his way.

Whether it was the Tuskers or coincidence, there were a couple of places along the road that a car couldn't have passed: a toppled tree, a rockslide. The bike made it around them easily. They passed the road to Pederson's barn, and Barry looked over at it. It was as tall and imposing as ever, like a fortress.

I'm going to bring Jenny and Barbara back here, he decided. He wasn't sure how Pederson would feel about it, but he'd dare him to turn them away. He had a feeling the old man wouldn't even if he wanted to.

They went by the burned-out SUV and trailer, which were almost unrecognizable, just blackened husks of metal. The trailer was as burned as the car, and Barry was glad he hadn't made his last stand there.

His heart lifted as he curved around the last few turns to his house. At the same time, he was as frightened as he'd ever been since the whole thing had started, more scared than when he'd been surrounded by Tuskers. What if something had happened? What if…what if they'd gotten to her?

He heard the shot before he saw the javelina. Barbara had seen it rushing from the side of the road and calmly shot it between the eyes. But it was like a signal to the others because suddenly, they were all over the place.

They drove into Barry's driveway. The house looked like it had been shelled. There were holes everywhere, the innards of the rooms dragged out onto what was left of the lawn and savaged. Pure, mean-hearted vandalism.

He pulled up to the door, got off the motorcycle, and drew his gun. The bike sprang up as Barbara dismounted. They stood back to back, surrounded.

Chapter Twenty-Nine

And then the strangest thing happened. They were surrounded, but when Barbara started walking to the door, the javelinas pulled back. Nervously, not understanding what was going on, Barry followed.

A Tusker came from inside the house. It was not one he'd seen before, but he recognized it for what it was. It had a broad, white stripe down its back.

Stripe, Barry thought. *His name is Stripe.*

Stripe grunted urgent orders, and a few of the pigs responded and started forward aggressively. But the rest ignored him. When the more obedient ones saw that the rest of their kind were holding back, they stopped. Barbara walked to the door, and Barry could swear the animals were bowing to her. She opened it up and stepped inside.

He followed her up the stairs.

They had tried hard to get in. The metal sheet was dented and even punctured in a few places, but it had held. The pigs had also dug into the walls, and each of the holes was surrounded by dried blood. His wife had closed each of the holes with wood from inside the room though he was having a hard time imagining what she'd used.

They stood before the door, and Barbara reached out and gently knocked on the metal.

"Who is it?" The voice was harsh, and Barry barely recognized it.

"It's me, babe," he said.

"Oh, God!" Jenny cried. "You made it. Oh, thank God…"

This is where they should have been hugging, but there was

a flaw in Barry's plan. "Uh, how do I get in?"

"I'll pull the nails away," Jenny said eagerly. He heard a screeching sound as she put the claw of the hammer under one of the nail heads and starting levering it out.

He looked down the stairs, expecting a rush of the enemy, but there wasn't a creature to be seen. There was more squeaking, and a small gap opened on one side, and he could see his wife's excited, green eyes looking out. He stuck his finger in the gap and felt her tug on it.

Eventually, she pulled out enough nails for him to push the metal aside enough to squeeze in. Jenny gave him a quick hug then pushed him away and started picking up nails and the hammer. "Hi, I'm Jenny," she said to Barbara, who came in after Barry, as if she didn't recognize her.

"I know, dear. I'm Barbara Weiss, remember me?"

"Barbara? You look…different." Jenny started hammering the wood back in place.

There was a whining sound, and Barry felt something rub up against his leg. It was Aragorn. He was limping; his left front leg seemed to be missing a chunk. But he seemed happy to see Barry.

"Arie saved my life a few times," Jenny said and stopped her hammering long enough to pet him on the head. He flopped over and showed his tummy.

"Stop hammering, babe," Barry said. "We're leaving."

"Leaving?" she said as if she couldn't believe it. "But we're safe here."

Barry didn't say anything, but it was clear that the struggle here had been desperate and that it had been a near thing. "How much food do you have?" he asked. "How much water?"

"Enough water to last a few days," she answered stubbornly. "And we still have plenty of food."

Barry looked around the room. It was a slightly neater version of what he'd seen at Barbara's. Everything that could be taken apart and nailed up had been dismantled. He noticed a stink coming from the bathroom and could only imagine that Jenny had stopped flushing the toilet. The dog looked famished.

"We don't know how long it will take for the rescuers to get to us," he said. "We're off the beaten path."

"But we're surrounded," she said. "We *can't* get away."

"We got in," he pointed out. Barry went over to his wife, took her by the elbow, and led her off to one side.

"I think they're afraid of her," he said, nodding over toward Barbara.

The sheriff had a serene look on her face, as if she was enjoying a pleasant visit with friends.

"What's wrong with her?" Jenny whispered.

"She fought them to the death," he said. "And she beat them. But…I think she's lost it."

"Where will we go?"

"Lyle Pederson is more prepared than any of us. He's got a near fortress, completely stocked. Enough weapons to fight World War III."

"Is the car outside?"

That stopped him. He hadn't thought of that. The poor motorcycle had nearly given out under the weight of Barbara and him. And what was he going to do with the dog?

"We'll have to make two trips," he said. "I've got a motorcycle."

In her expression, Barry saw the total rejection of his plan. She picked up the hammer again and reached for a nail. "I'm not leaving Arie behind."

Barry was not sure what would have happened then if Barbara hadn't spoken up. "Your husband is right," she said. "You should listen to your husband."

Great, he thought. *The crazy, lonely lady speaks.* But when Barry looked into her face, he saw an awareness there that he hadn't seen since he'd found her.

"They will keep coming until they get you or until you've killed them all," Barbara said. "Killed so many of them that your soul leaves your body and you become a monster. You don't want that."

Barry shuddered, and he could see the truth of her words get through to Jenny.

"I'll take care of Arie," Barbara said. "I promise."

The other two just stood there, staring at her.

"Go!" The sheriff's command voice was back, and they both jumped. "Get out of here before more of the Mean Ones come. I've cowed the javelinas, but the Mean Ones will get me eventually. But not before I've taken a few more of them out."

Barry took Jenny by the shoulders and led her to the door. She dropped to her knees near Aragorn and gave him one last hug. Then she turned back to Barbara.

"Are you sure?"

"It's for the best, dear," the sheriff said, her matronly voice returning. "Now go!"

Barry pulled his gun from his belt and led the way. He saw Jenny's eyes go wide at the sight of the pistol but ignored it. They started down the stairs. Arie started to follow them.

Jenney turned and raised a finger. "Stay."

The dog whined but stopped on the top step.

Barry heard footsteps behind him, and Barbara pushed past them and led the way.

There must have been a hundred javelinas outside, but once again, they parted for the sheriff. Jenny and Barry got on the bike, feeling awed.

Barry started the engine and looked back. Barbara raised her hand once then turned and went back inside. He roared out of the driveway before the pigs could realize that their nemesis was gone.

Barbara had known some retired law enforcement officers who had swallowed their guns. That had always been inexplicable to her. It had never occurred to her that she might be one of them.

In her case, she wasn't actually doing it herself. She was daring the Tuskers to do it.

That was her secret. It was why she'd been so fearless; it was what the poor javelinas had seen in her eyes—an utter lack of caring what happened to her.

As she waited for Barry to return, she felt hope coming back, and with it came fear.

She wished she could have told the Hunters not to worry about her. Not to risk their lives coming back for her. But she knew that they would have delayed, hesitated, debated about what to do next. So she'd just agreed, suspecting that Barry would return too late.

When she'd walked among the javelinas, she'd looked into the eyes of the Tusker Barry called Stripe. There had been no awe there. No respect. Just hate.

She knew then that the Mean One was figuring out a way to get her.

She sat on the floor of the Hunters' bedroom. There was no furniture left intact except the bed, and it seemed wrong to her to sit there. She rubbed Arie's ears, and he looked up at her with sad eyes as if he understood what she was thinking.

"Sorry, boy," she said. "I don't think either of us are getting out of here. But I couldn't let them die trying to save you. You're what, twelve years old? You and me have had a good life, right, boy? But maybe it's time for us to move on."

Barbara paused then kept talking aloud. She was pretty sure she was crazy. At the very least, she was suffering from PTSD.

"I've never been religious, but for some reason, I think you're listening to this, Howard. When you died, I thought my life was over. Then…I thought maybe I could go on.

"But I was right the first time."

She looked up at the metal door the Hunters had created and wondered if she should nail it shut. But she couldn't be bothered.

She checked her clip. Four bullets left.

Arie was still looking at her. "Don't worry, boy. I'll save one for you and one for me. But I'd like to take out at least one more of these bastards."

So they waited, and the time was pleasant. It seemed to pass slowly, so unlike the past five years after Howard had died, which had passed in what seemed days. Maybe she was crazy, but in many ways, she was more herself than she'd been as Miss Feminine Man-Hungry.

She shuddered. *How embarrassing.* Then she laughed.

Looks like I'll die of embarrassment.

She heard a noise at the bottom of the stairs.

"Ready?" she whispered to Arie, who wagged his tail and put his head in her lap. Barbara didn't even bother to get up from her cross-legged position.

A javelina ran in, one of the normals, and she shot it. It was supposed to be a distraction, she sensed.

These Tuskers were too damn smart. But she had thirty years of cop instincts, and that trumped them.

The Tusker came in right after the normal one, and she aimed for its eyes and saw the recognition in them, the surprise in the creature as it realized it was going to die. She nailed it from just inches away, and it slid the rest of the way over to her. Arie jumped up for a second then came back to her.

There was more movement outside, which meant there was at least one more Tusker.

Barbara turned the gun on Arie, who didn't flinch.

"Sorry, boy," she said as she shot him in the side of the head.

Then she put the gun to her own temple. The last thing she ever saw was three Tuskers charging her.

Chapter Thirty

"No," Lyle Pederson said when Barry told him they'd come to hunker down and that he needed to return to his house to get Barbara and Arie.

"What you mean, *no*?"

"I mean no, you can't hunker down here."

Barry was too stunned to speak.

Jenny took umbrage for him. "And just where are we supposed to go, Mr. Pederson?"

"Call me Lyle."

She stared at him in disbelief then sniffed. "It doesn't sound like I'm going to get to know you well enough for first names, *Mr.* Pederson. Come on, Barry. We're not going to beg. We survived perfectly fine at *our* house."

Perfectly fine? Barry looked around at the reinforced walls of the barn, the stacks of supplies, the unlocked and open gun cabinet bristling with ordinance. In comparison, their house looked like it would fall over in the first strong winter storm.

"You misunderstand me, Jen...Mrs. Hunter," Pederson said. "I said you couldn't *hunker down* here. I didn't say you couldn't stay as long as you do your part."

"And what would that be, Mr. Pederson?"

"We aren't waiting for rescue. We're taking the fight to the Tuskers."

Barry spoke up. "Seems to me that we've been fighting the Tuskers all along, and so far, we've been having our asses kicked."

"That's because we've been hunkering down," Pederson

said, unperturbed. "They know where to find us. They know our weaknesses. Look at you, Barry. You've been a wild card, brave and smart enough to get out and see what's happening while everyone else has just been hiding their heads in the sand. Hasn't worked out too well for most of them."

Jenny started to object, but Barry put his hand on her arm. "He might be right, Jenny."

Barry told them about Peggy and Mark, who'd been set up in the perfect spot and had still been killed. Then he told them about Barbara and what he'd found at her house.

"She may have been *defending* her home," Barry said. "But she was doing it in the most *offensive*-minded way possible."

"And now the pigs are scared of her," Jenny said. "I swear to God, they looked like they were worshipping some kind of war goddess or something."

"Just goes to prove my point," Pederson said. "We have to show them that we won't simply wait to be slaughtered. That we are going to be unpredictable. That they have to look over their shoulders just like we do."

He picked up an assault rifle. "This is an AK-47. I've modified it to fully automatic. Let's see how those swine do under a hail of bullets."

Barry looked at Jenny, letting her decide.

"Lyle," she said, and he grinned. "You've got a deal."

What she said next surprised the hell out of Barry. "We've got to fight back," she continued. "We have to defeat them at their own game. We should be able to do that! We've been the masters of this world for decades, centuries; hell, millennia. We've outsmarted everything thrown against us, including Mother Nature herself. Fuck us if we can't defeat a bunch of skunk pigs."

"Fuck us?" Barry echoed.

"Yeah," she said defiantly. "Fuck us."

"Well, I like the sentiment, Jenny," Lyle said. "But we don't want to get too cocky. I think that's what got us in trouble in the first place."

Jenny looked slightly chastened, but Barry grinned at her, and she quickly regained her swagger: Jenny, who had contemplated not paying taxes because she didn't want to pay for wars. *Strange times*, Barry mused.

She turned to him. "You'd better get back to the house, Barry. I'm worried about Arie…and Barbara."

Barry climbed back on the bike.

"Wait a minute, son," Pederson said. He came over with two fresh clips. "I'm guessing you're a little on the low side."

"Thanks…Lyle."

Barry knew it was useless before he turned the last corner. He could see smoke on the horizon. There were pigs limping down the road, looking up at him as he drove by. They didn't even attempt to stop him.

The yard was swarming with javelinas. It looked like they were having some kind of celebration. There, on top of the mailbox, was a human head, which they were dancing around.

At the base of the post, Barry saw Aragorn's golden fur.

Barbara's face was still calm. Her eyes seemed to have that same flatness he remembered, but now, they were filming over in death.

He stopped the motorcycle a good distance away. There were three Tuskers standing on the porch, overlooking the dance of death. *That explains it*, Barry thought. Even Barbara wasn't a match for three of them. All of them had blood on their muzzles. He recognized Stripe and perhaps Vader; the third one, he didn't know. How many of them were there? Pederson—Lyle—had figured there'd been a single litter of the genius pigs. How many pigs were in a litter? Seemed to Barry that he'd read they could be pretty big. *Sometimes as many as a dozen*, he thought.

The Tuskers were grunting commands. The javelinas were starting to face his direction.

Barry thought about what Lyle had said about the humans being on the run, being defensive, always being predictable. He drew his gun with his left hand and revved the engine with his right hand and pretended to start turning the bike around. He waited until the cadre of pigs started running toward him then charged them, shooting a path through them as he went.

The three Tuskers were frozen in surprise, and Barry was only yards away from them when they finally started to move. He figured he had at least six bullets left and another clip ready to go. The javelinas had all overshot him and were scrambling to turn around. He had a second or two.

He took aim at Stripe and blew his head off. A mist of blood blew over Stripe's brothers (or sisters). Then he aimed at Vader, but the Tusker was already dodging back into the house. The third Tusker was slightly slower, so he shot at it instead and saw it limping by the time it reached the doorway.

Then Barry turned his bike around and rode down the side of the house and found the trail he sometimes used to hike down to the road.

He was gone before they knew it.

That night, they sat in the bright light provided by the generators and pondered their next move.

"You were right, Lyle," Barry said. "They had no clue that I wouldn't run. That I would actually dare attack them."

Lyle was polishing his AK-47. "Did you know the term 'assault rifle' originated with Hitler?" he said.

What could they say to that? Barry thought it wasn't a coincidence that Lyle had first called Razorback "the Leader," or that he had called one of the brood Himmler.

Lyle got up abruptly and walked off then came back with a bottle of vodka and three glasses. He poured them each a couple of fingers. "To Barbara Weiss, warrior woman," he toasted.

They all took a drink.

"To Barbara, the widow who just wanted to start a new life," Jenny said. They finished off the vodka, and Lyle poured them another round.

"To Peggy and Mark," Barry said.

They silently took a drink.

"Those poor kids," Barry said. "I really thought they were safe. It was incredibly unlucky their building caught fire."

"I don't think bad luck had anything to do with it," Lyle said.

That took a moment to penetrate. "What, you think the Tuskers did it? That they can start fires?"

"You haven't been listening to me, Barry. These aren't just really smart pigs. They're way beyond that. I think they might be smarter than we are."

"You can't be serious."

"Think about it. You and me and everyone else in this valley have thousands of years of culture and technology behind us. We have tools and weapons. These Tuskers can't have been around all that long, yet...look who's winning."

Barry didn't have a response to that.

"Lyle?" Jenny said. "Maybe I should call you 'Mr. Pederson' with this question. But really...don't you think help is on the way? I can't imagine it will take much longer."

Lyle nodded. "Good question. Answer is, I can't imagine it either. I'll be very surprised if rescue teams haven't arrived by noon tomorrow. I've been monitoring my CB, and it sounds like a massive effort is underway. They even seem to understand that there is some kind of wild animal epidemic. I've heard the word 'rabies,' which means they'll be on the lookout for aggressive animals."

"So Mr. Pederson. Why don't we hunker down?" Jenny waved around her at the barn. "It would take an army of genius pigs to figure out a way to get in here, and they'd be met by—as you put it—a 'hail of bullets.'"

"That's why we have to hurry," Lyle said.

"I don't understand," Jenny said.

"I think we have to kill them all off," Lyle said. "I don't believe we can let any of the Tuskers escape."

"Kill them all off," Jenny echoed quietly.

"You're talking about genocide," Barry objected.

"No, I'm talking about the survival of our species. If these Tuskers can do this much damage in such a short time, think what they might accomplish given more time, more experience, more of a chance to develop their own technology."

"Oh, come on."

"I'm serious. So far, everything that supposedly makes us superior, they've been able to match except for maybe the opposable thumb thingy. If they figure out a way around that, well, who knows?"

"Look, I don't like the Tuskers any more than you do. But you've got to have some sneaking admiration for them."

"Oh, I do. More than you, apparently. And it's exactly that attitude that's going to be the end of us. The authorities will figure out that these Tuskers are something different pretty fast, I suspect. They'll want to capture them, study them."

"What's wrong with that?" Jenny asked. "We can keep them contained. Maybe teach them some manners."

Lyle laughed. "I just had an image of a bunch of Neanderthals sitting around a fire, drinking fermented apple juice and saying the same thing about us."

Chapter Thirty-One

The next morning, Barry awoke filled with doubt about their tactics. He didn't know how they were going to accomplish wiping out the Tuskers, but he suspected Lyle had a plan.

It wasn't only that they were contemplating the genocide of an apparently new species, it was also his own motivation for doing it. He was afraid what he wanted was revenge: for Barbara, and Peggy and Mark, and for the Silversteins and all the others.

He thought Lyle was overstating the Tuskers' intelligence. Sure, they were canny beasts, but genius level? What did that even mean? It was laughable that humans couldn't control a bunch of pigs no matter how smart those pigs were.

He could see the same doubt in Jenny's eyes. She sidled up to him. "We can try to delay him," she whispered. "The cops will be here any moment. It's not only that I think it's utterly immoral and despicable to wipe out an entire species—a new species at that—but it sounds fucking dangerous."

"Jeez, Jenny. You're really liking that swear word all of a sudden."

"Sorry," she blushed. "But really. We're just a couple of retired white-collar workers. What business is it of ours?"

Barry totally agreed. "We'll drag our feet. See what happens."

They'd slept on a couple of cots toward the center of the barn while Lyle had camped out in a small office he had to one side. Now, their host came bustling out of the office, dressed in army fatigues, a holster on his belt.

Jenny looked at Barry with raised eyebrows.

"Come over here, you two," Lyle said. He sounded painfully

cheerful to Barry's morning ears.

"You got any coffee?" Barry asked.

He pointed to the office. "Already brewed. All I got is black though."

Black was just what Barry needed: a bitter jolt of caffeine.

"Grab me a cup, too, honey," Jenny said. It was Barry's turn to raise his eyebrows because she usually drank tea.

When they both had cups in hand, Lyle said, "All set?"

Barry shook his head. "Give me some time to wake up, Lyle. I'm useless without a couple cups of coffee."

He drank his coffee as slowly as he could then went and got another cup. Lyle busied himself at the workbench for a time, but he was getting more and more impatient. Finally, he snapped, "No more lollygagging. Get over here, and check out this map. Both of you."

He'd brushed aside all the high-tech-looking gadgets on his workbench and unfolded a big piece of paper. It was a topographical map of the valley.

He pointed to a spot on the map near where he had the barn marked in red. "This is a little box canyon at the back of my property. It's where I store my propane tanks. I've got a real fear of propane, I got to tell you. I had a friend get terribly burned once…" His voice trailed off, and then he visibly shook off the memory.

"I've rigged the propane tanks to explode and added other fuels to make it burn even hotter. It will fill that canyon with a fireball that no one…no pig…can survive. It will be something to behold—as long as you're at a distance.

"Anyway, I've noticed that the Tuskers like to hide in the canyon in the heat of the day. I've even observed Razorback going in there a few times, and I've been tempted to blow him up when I had the chance. But I want to get them *all*."

He turned to Barry with the glittering eyes of a fanatic. "*All* the Tuskers. It was something you said, Barry, that got me thinking. You mentioned that you thought that maybe killing off Razorback would be enough to stop the other pigs. Well, we know now that Razorback might be head pig, but his offspring are perfectly capable of taking over.

"But what would happen if we managed to kill Razorback while the others were watching? What if the person who did the killing was close enough to entice them to follow?"

Jenny spoke up. "What if that person led the rest of them into the canyon?"

"Exactly! *Boom!* Tuskers are history."

Barry didn't say anything. That was a whole lot of "what ifs." Real life didn't work that way. Too many things could go wrong, the biggest being…

Jenny had also spotted the flaw. "What happens to the Judas goat?" she asked. "Does he—or she—go boom too?"

Lyle's enthusiasm didn't diminish. "Well, that's tricky. But it can be done." He pointed to the map. "There's a trail at the back of the canyon. You can't see it unless you know it's there. I'm pretty sure that a man can get up it, but a pig would have more trouble."

"These are javelinas, Lyle," Barry pointed out. "They're like mountain goats."

"Nah, it only looks that way. Actually, all the steep hills you see them on? They've totally grooved trails into them. With a real vertical climb, they're pretty hapless."

They all fell silent for a few moments, staring at the map. Jenny and Barry managed not to look at each other, but Barry knew they were thinking the same thing. It was a crazy, dangerous plan, and there was no way they wanted to be part of it. They had to figure out a way to slow Lyle down long enough for the helicopters to arrive or the all-terrain vehicles or whatever the rescuers were using to get to them. It couldn't be long now.

Barry didn't want to die when they were on the verge of being saved.

He glanced at Lyle…and he had an image of a skinny, white-haired Captain Ahab. Lyle was ready to kill them all because of some vendetta, some cockamamie theory about survival of the species.

"I have to pee," Jenny announced. She headed for the back, and there was an uneasy silence as the two men waited for her to come back. She was taking a long time. Barry knew she was trying to stall.

"What if…?" he started to ask.

"If you don't mind, I'd like us all to be here when we discuss our plans," Lyle said.

Barry fell silent. Jenny was probably pushing it. He'd planned to announce he needed to piss too right after she got back, but he could tell Lyle would see right through the delay.

Jenny returned, walking slowly. "So," she said. "Who's the goat?"

At first, Lyle didn't answer…which in itself gave Barry the answer.

"Look," Lyle said finally, sounding apologetic. "I'd do it, but I can't drive a motorcycle, and I don't think I can outrun the damn pigs. It pretty much *has* to be you, Barry."

"No," Jenny said. It was her flat voice, the one Barry had learned not to argue with. She'd made up her mind, and that was that.

He shrugged helplessly at Lyle.

Suddenly, all Lyle's folksy friendliness disappeared. His face was a mask, his eyes hard gems. "Get out," he said.

"Lyle…" Barry began.

"No!" he shouted. "I know what you're trying to do. You've been delaying all morning. Well, if you aren't going to pull your weight around here, you can just get out."

Jenny and Barry exchanged shocked glances. Then she nodded. "Can we take the guns, at least?"

"Of course," Lyle said.

They started for the door. The motorcycle was just inside it, fueled and ready to go. The last thing Barry remembered seeing before going to bed was Lyle giving it a tune-up. The engine roared in the confines of the barn, and he could tell from the revving that it was going to have more power than before.

Jenny checked the window then opened the door.

Barry started to drive through.

"Hold on!" he heard. He turned to see Lyle walking toward them, his face red, a gun in his hand. Barry almost reached for his own weapon.

"You can stay," Lyle shouted.

Jenny slammed the door, and Barry turned off the engine.

Lyle looked embarrassed. "I'm sorry. If you don't want to do this, that's your right. But would you at least teach me how to drive the motorcycle?"

"Shit," Barry said.

He saw Jenny stiffen, and he knew that she had already figured out what he was going to say. But what else could he do? This old man had saved his life more than once. Without the weapon Lyle had given him, he would have been pig shit a long time ago. The man had fed them and sheltered them and showed them every kindness.

He couldn't let the old man commit suicide. Sure, Pederson could probably learn the rudiments of riding a motorcycle in a short time, but over the past couple of days, Barry had gotten pretty good at it. He kinda flattered himself that he was a natural. *If I survive this*, he thought, *I might just take up the sport.* That and target practice, which (he also flattered himself) he was better at than most. They were much better duffer sports than pickleball and noodling, that's for sure.

"Barry…" Jenny said warningly.

He got off the bike.

"All right, Lyle. Show me your plan again…and this time, be specific. Where do I find Razorback, and how do I get the other Tuskers to follow me?"

Chapter Thirty-Two

The more detailed the plan became, the more comfortable Barry became with it. He realized that was probably delusional, his brain rationalizing the craziness. His initial reaction was probably the more reliable one.

Lyle had marked the places on the map where each of the Tuskers hung out. "I've counted eight Tuskers still surviving, counting Razorback," he said. "Each of them have their favorite spots, but not many are that close together. I'm thinking there is some sibling rivalry going on. However, Vader and Attila are usually together, and so are Thatcher and Reagan."

"Why, Lyle. I do believe you are a closet liberal," Jenny laughed.

His face reddened as if Jenny had touched a nerve. He drew a route on the map from where Razorback's hiding place was to the next hiding spot then to the next. "You'll have to go slow enough to let them follow but fast enough to not let them catch you," he warned Barry.

That sounded easy; the kind of easy that was actually incredibly hard.

"What if they don't follow me?" Barry asked.

Lyle shrugged. "Then my plan didn't work. You've had a nice motorcycle ride, and we wait for rescue. But if you can kill Razorback first, that will make the whole thing worth it. And if you can get even one of the Tuskers to follow you, then I'll consider it a great success."

Lyle stood up. "Come on, both of you."

He led them over to and then up the spiral staircase. Jenny gasped at the view from the top. "I wish I'd gotten to know you sooner, Lyle," she said.

"Me too," he said, patting her back in a fatherly way.

He picked up a metal box that was sitting on the chair next to the telescope. "This is the trigger. From this vantage point, I'm pretty sure nothing can obscure the signal."

"Pretty sure?" Barry asked.

"Well, without blowing up the propane, I can't be totally sure. But again, if the plan doesn't work, it doesn't work."

Except I will have risked my life for nothing, Barry thought, but he didn't say anything out loud.

Lyle handed to switch to Jenny. "That will be your job, Jenny. When you see that Barry has climbed safely out of the canyon, you flip the switch."

"Me?" she exclaimed. "What are you going to be doing?"

"Someone has to close the gate to the box canyon after the Tuskers have followed Barry in. The moment I drop the gate, I'll be running for my life, so don't you hesitate to pull the trigger when the time comes."

He twirled the telescope around and sighted it in. "Barry, check the canyon out. Familiarize yourself with it. There is a single fir tree in the back. Directly behind it is the path out. It is pretty steep, I warn you. I've hung a rope down, so that ought to help."

Barry examined the area. He saw the tree; he even thought he could see the rope. "Seems simple enough."

"When things get dangerous, even simple tasks can become difficult," Lyle said. "So I've tried to make everything as easy as possible. The only complicated part is getting the damn Tuskers to follow you. So with that in mind, I'd like you to use the telescope to trace your route."

He positioned the telescope again and grunted in satisfaction. "Razorback is in his usual spot, surrounded by his harem. If you come down the trail from above, he won't hear you until it's too late. I'm pretty sure you can get a shot."

Lyle pulled a gun from a holster at the small of his back and handed it to Barry. Barry looked at it curiously; it appeared to be exactly the same type of gun he was carrying.

"It's an automatic," Lyle explained. "It's also got twenty-two rounds instead of fifteen, so watch out: it's just the slightest bit heavier. When you point it at old Razorback, you can empty the entire clip with one pull of the trigger. Try to track him because even the slightest recoil can send the bullets flying over his head. We'll practice-shoot a clip downstairs before you leave."

Then they all grew quiet. Barry checked his watch. The whole planning session hadn't taken more than half an hour. It was still early morning.

Barry turned to Jenny. "You might as well stay here," he said. Before he was finished speaking, she'd jumped into his arms, and he felt her rest her lips against his neck and heard her whisper, "Don't do anything stupid. Just run if the plan falls apart, okay?"

"Don't worry. First thing that goes wrong, I'm outta there."

Barry turned to descend the staircase. Jenny had her hand on the end of the telescope, and he realized that she would be watching the whole thing as it happened. He almost wished she couldn't because no matter what he said, he knew that most plans didn't survive exposure to reality.

The motorcycle nearly purred it was so well tuned. It gave Barry great comfort to know that he had such power beneath him.

Unlike the sleek lines of the bike, he felt bulky. Lyle had fashioned him some stiff leather leggings. "I think these will withstand even the Tusker's tusks," he said, strapping them onto Barry.

"I won't be able run very well," Barry said dubiously.

"If you have to run, Barry, you're already dead. When you reach the path, you just flip these clips here, and the leggings will fall away."

Barry got on the bike. Lyle handed him a small revolver. "Here, stick this in your pocket." He stood back and examined Barry then held up a finger for him to wait, went over to the gun locker, and came back with the biggest knife Barry had ever seen. Lyle attached it to Barry's belt. "*Now* you're ready," he said.

They shook hands, and then Barry was off.

There were a few javelinas outside, and they were caught off guard by Barry's sudden appearance. He suspected they were only there as observers. It occurred to him that he was thinking of Tuskers the way he would have thought of a human enemy. *Except*, he thought, *they might be smarter.*

He headed up the foothills to the east of Razorback's hiding place. He would be coming west down a steep trail that flattened out right as it reached the base of the gully. From there, Lyle had assured him, he should have a clean shot.

Then he was supposed to slap in another clip and keep going down the same trail, where another hiding place was also visible, and empty another clip. After that, well, the trick would be keeping out of the Tuskers' reach while staying close enough to lure them the rest of the way into the box canyon.

Easy, right?

Barry didn't have much time to think, which was fortunate. On the way, he rehearsed the path in his mind, and for a while, it was exactly as he imagined.

Then he turned the corner and came upon Razorback's lair.

The giant Tusker wasn't lying back in the shade, surrounded by other javelinas. He was standing in the middle of the trail as if expecting Barry.

Barry had the gun in his hand. He lowered it and pulled the trigger.

The Tusker jumped to his left, down a steep incline, and tumbled out of sight. Barry wasn't sure he'd hit him even once. At least half the bullets had gone over his head despite Barry's best effort to control the recoil.

He stopped to put in the second clip and craned his neck to see over the edge of the incline, but Razorback was nowhere in sight. There were rocks and bushes everywhere. There were a few splatters of blood too, and that gave him some hope.

He heard the sound of pursuit and took off again. The next gully was more like what he'd envisioned. The two Tuskers that Lyle had named Reagan and Thatcher were just getting to their feet. Barry emptied the second clip into them, and he was pretty sure he killed them both.

He tossed the automatic away and cranked the motorcycle, and the back tires kicked rocks and dust into the faces of the pursuing pigs.

The one element of the plan he'd thought was the most

unpredictable seemed to be working. When he looked back, it seemed as if every javelina in the county—hell, the *world*—was coming after him. At their head, he saw four bigger ones: Tuskers, he hoped. So that was six out of eight Tuskers accounted for if he included Razorback.

In his pocket, Barry had the small revolver that Lyle had handed him at the last moment, which held six rounds. But that wasn't going to save him for long. In fact, the bike was the only thing saving him, and he was having a hard time settling on the right speed. He'd slow down, and it would seem as if the javelinas were exhilarated and were only feet away before he sped up again. Then he'd lose sight of them and worry that they'd quit pursuing him, which was the point of the whole plan, after all.

Finally, he realized that if he mostly coasted in neutral and gave the bike an occasional burst of speed, he'd be traveling at the same speed as the sprinting pigs. After a while of this, he saw the red, overhanging rock that was the signpost that he was nearly at the box canyon.

But the overhang also hid one of the missing Tuskers. He came at Barry from the side before he could swerve, and he felt a tusk rip into his leggings. The leather that had seemed so secure that he'd been worried about removing it tore off of one leg and went flying. The momentum spun the Tusker around, and his flank caught the rear tire, and suddenly, Barry was tumbling head over heels.

The natural tendency when falling is to put out your hands, which in this case would have been an invitation for a broken arm. Instead, Barry tucked and rolled. He was reaching for the revolver before he'd stopped tumbling. He pulled it out and started firing wildly even before he saw where the Tusker was coming from. By sheer luck, one of the bullets blew off the Tusker's right front leg. It was still hobbling toward him as he was getting to his feet. He presented it with the leg that was still covered by leather, drew the huge bowie knife, and charged the Tusker, which surprised it long enough for Barry to plunge the knife deep into the creature's side.

It squealed and died.

Just like any other pig, Barry thought.

He looked up. The other Tuskers had simply been watching; for whatever reason, they hadn't come to their sibling's aid. But now, they charged.

Barry lifted the bike, kicked it into gear, and rode away.

Right away, he could tell something was wrong. The motorcycle was no longer a dream machine but a bucking bronco. Every few hundred feet, it seemed to slow down a little more.

He decided that keeping the pursuers in teasing sight was no longer necessary and built up as much speed as he could. By the time the bike sputtered to a stop at the base of the hill, the box canyon was in sight. Barry could hear his pursuers but could no longer see them. He didn't think it would take them long to catch up though.

He reached down and unhooked what was left of his leggings. Then he started running, shedding his leather coat, the empty revolver, and everything else he could. He held the bowie knife in one hand though it probably wouldn't do him much good if he was swarmed.

He was only a few yards from the canyon when Razorback emerged from the bushes. Barry ran past him without hesitating, and that seemed to catch the Tusker by surprise. *What, does he think I'm going to fight him head on?* Barry thought.

Razorback quickly recovered from his surprise and came after Barry. If the Tusker was injured, he was showing no signs of it. From a distance, the canyon had looked tiny, but now, the back of it seemed impossibly distant. The fir tree was beckoning, but Barry could hear Razorback close behind him.

He turned with bowie knife in hand, knowing it was an impossible fight.

Lyle Pederson came out of nowhere and somehow managed to get between the charging pig and Barry. He had his Glock, and he fired all twenty rounds in seconds. Razorback kept coming, and then his head reared up, his tusks catching Lyle right in the belly, and blood and viscera went everywhere.

Lyle didn't make a sound as he fell.

Barry turned and ran. He wanted to stop. He wanted to help.

But he knew Lyle was dead. If Barry was killed too, it would all be for nothing. He felt scared, and he felt a sudden sense of loss. He wondered why all this was happening. It couldn't be real... could it?

But the blood running down the Tusker's chest was real, as was his deep grunting. Razorback keep rumbling after him for a few yards then stumbled. The Tusker skidded to his knees and stayed there, panting. Barry was still moving, but he was stumbling backward because he couldn't take his eyes off the dying animal.

Razorback's Tusker offspring arrived and all the lesser javelinas. They milled around their leader. Then Vader walked up to his father and sniffed him.

He lunged toward Razorback's neck, his curled tusks digging in deeply, and with a last roar, the giant pig fell over and died.

Then Vader turned his yellow eyes toward Barry.

Barry turned and ran in pure panic. The rope was only feet away, and despite his fatigue, he found a surge of energy and jumped as high up it as he could get. It burned his hands as he fought for purchase, but finally, he stopped sliding. Then his feet were scrabbling for footholds, and he was pulling himself out of reach.

Or so he thought.

He looked down to see the three surviving Tuskers with their heads together almost as if they were conferring. One of them broke off and started running for the cliff, and Barry had the wild thought that the thing was going to jump up and get him.

The Tusker only made it about half the distance, and a huge relief washed over Barry. He hung there and looked out at the canyon. It was full of javelinas. The humans needn't have worried about fencing them in. They weren't going anywhere. They were watching their Tusker leaders.

Barry's relief was short-lived because the second Tusker jumped, and it balanced on the first Tusker's neck and thrust itself further up the rope just inches from Barry's feet.

Vader was last, and as Barry saw him gather his strength

for a mighty leap, he started desperately pulling himself up the rope, his feet slipping on the rocks, his hands slippery with blood.

Vader seemed to come flying straight at him but then started to fall. Even so, he caught himself on the second Tusker's shoulders and thrust himself upward again.

"Pigs...don't....fly!" Barry screamed, and he pushed off from the cliff and kicked Vader with all his might. He felt a tusk penetrate his foot, but he also felt the force of his kick pushing the Tusker away, and Vader went tumbling down on top of the other Tuskers, and then they all were falling.

Barry was only inches from the top of the cliff, but it took all his energy to pull himself over the lip. There was a downhill slope on the other side, and he tumbled down it, unable to stop himself.

He lay there for a moment, spitting out dirt.

And then the ground seemed to lift up underneath him, and he felt a pressure in his ears, and a huge, glorious fireball rose above him as if he was lying in the middle of Hiroshima, and he had a moment to wonder at the beauty of it before rocks the size of his head started coming down on him. He briefly saw a shadow pass over him and then saw no more.

Chapter Thirty-Three

Barry awoke inside a helicopter. He regained consciousness long enough to realize that and to see a concerned-looking medic in a uniform looking down at him, and then he was out again.

The next time he awoke, he was in a hospital, and Jenny was sitting beside him.

"Did we…" Barry croaked. His mouth was so dry he could barely speak.

"Hush, honey," she said. "You're safe."

"Lyle?"

She shook her head, and then Barry remembered Razorback bowling the old man over, flinging him into the air.

All gone in a blaze of fire.

t took days for the authorities to figure out what happened—or at least to arrive at a coherent story they could live with: a rabies outbreak, some kind of virulent new form that had affected only the javelinas.

Strangely, they could find only a few surviving skunk pigs. Most of them had been destroyed—by coincidence, apparently— by an accidental propane explosion. The few javelinas they could find had tested as normal.

Most of the uproar in the news was over how long it had taken for the emergency teams to arrive. Lots of fingers were pointed, but no one took the fall.

On Lyle Pederson's workbench, the authorities found his last will and testament. Somehow, Lyle had managed to change his will in the midst of all the chaos. It was even notarized, dated only the day before the final events of the crisis had unfolded.

Turned out Lyle had been worth even more money than Barry had thought. Along with the will, there was a handwritten message.

The note read:

Dear Jenny and Barry,

I hope you have survived our encounter with the Tuskers. Well, I suppose if you are reading this, at least one of you is alive, and I am dead.

Since I am dead, I can tell you that I wasn't just blowing hot air about the Tuskers. I do believe they are a danger to mankind.

As you can see, you've come into a great deal of money. I have no relatives, and few people I even like, and almost none that I admire and respect. I'd like to believe you became fond of me, and I appreciated that in my last days. And I do admire the courage you've both shown.

So it's all yours. Spend it, give it away; I don't care.

But I do have one request. This is not a legal requirement, for I know no judge would ever understand it much less uphold it. I'm giving you the money with no legal strings attached. So it is only your own consciences that will have to decide what to do with this request.

I want you to find out if we got them all. Every single Tusker. Because if we didn't, it won't be long before there are new litters of new Tuskers. I'm asking you to track down any survivors and kill them. Don't hesitate. Don't try to capture them.

Just kill them.

Thank you for coming into a lonely old man's life when he needed you most.

Lyle Pederson

Epilogue

Genghis was crossing the county line when the dust from the explosion drifted over him. The dust contained what was left of his father and all his siblings and all the Slow Ones who had followed them.

His father had made some mistakes. He had thought the Animal Control officer, Hamilton, was the enemy. They should have seen that Pederson was the true foe.

Genghis had snuck into the old man's high-tech barn more than once. He'd fiddled around with the old man's tools as best he could with his clumsy hooves. He'd even managed to fashion a few things by using leverage and clamps. But as long as humans had tools and The People did not, the humans would win.

His father had struck too soon. Even if he had managed to take over the ancestral territory of The People, more humans would have come from the outside. There had only been a single litter of the New Ones to lead The People, his brothers and sisters, and it hadn't been enough.

No, the thing to do was breed many litters everywhere. He'd discovered that the Slow Ones immediately recognized his supremacy and followed him. They could be pushed too far though. The crazy sheriff woman had shown that. He'd commanded what was left of his followers to attack, and they had refused.

Still, they acknowledged his dominance. He had his pick of the females. All of the females.

His sons and daughters would also have their pick, and their sons and daughters. They would grow their numbers in secrecy. No one would be allowed to reveal their true nature until their numbers were enough, until they had mastery of man's tools and the ability to use them.

The humans thought they had run into "smart" pigs. They had no idea that the New Ones were smarter than any human. More resourceful and cunning and ruthless.

At the county line, there was a fence. It was too high for Genghis to jump over. He looked up at the sign. "Welcome to Baker County, home of the jackalope."

The jackalope was some made-up creature, a jackrabbit with horns. The humans could be foolish sometimes. When he'd read their books, he'd had to ignore their flights of fancy to find the truth beneath.

There was a latched gate at one corner of the fence.

Genghis shrugged off the leather backpack he'd fashioned and rooted around for the tool he'd constructed. When he placed it on the end of his hoof, he could manage to create a crude approximation of an opposable thumb.

Curse the humans and their opposable thumbs, he thought. That was the only advantage they had. But they had taught him the importance of tools. Tools could do things that hands could not. So, too, tools could do things that hooves could not. It was only a matter of time before he built the tools that could build the tools that would defeat the humans. The humans were complacent, certain of their mastery, looking down on all the animals with claws and talons and hooves.

With his crude tool, Genghis reached up, grasped the latch, and opened the gate. He put the tool back in the pack and slithered into the straps.

He headed north toward the mountains, where The People were still wild and rarely encountered humans.

It's only a matter of time, Genghis vowed.

To be continued in:

TUSKERS II: DAY OF THE LONG PIG

About the Author

Duncan grew up and spent most of his life in Central Oregon, the dry side of the Cascades, and whose terrain is featured in many of his books. He wrote several books out of college, including the heroic fantasy novels Star Axe, Snowcastles, and Icetowers. In 1984, he and his wife Linda bought Pegasus Books in downtown Bend, Oregon, which they still own and operate. They also ran a used bookstore, the Bookmark, for 15 years.

In the last five years, he's been able to get back to writing again, and found that he has a lot of pent-up creative energy. He's written numerous books for several different publishers, mostly in the horror or dark fantasy genres, though recently has been branching out into fantasy again, as well as thrillers.

Curious about other Crossroad Press books?
Stop by our site:
http://store.crossroadpress.com
We offer quality writing
in digital, audio, and print formats.

Enter the code FIRSTBOOK
to get 20% off your first order from our store!
Stop by today!

.